MURDER,
HONEY

MURDER, HONEY

HONEY

Vinnie Hansen

Library of Congress Number: 99-90696
ISBN Numbers   Hardcover: 0-7388-0466-5
                 Softcover: 0-7388-0467-3

Cover photo courtesy of Paul Titangos.

"Death in the Open", copyright (c) 1973 by The Massachusetts Medical Society, from THE LIVES OF A CELL by Lewis Thomas. Used by permission of Viking Penguin, a division of Penguin Putnam Inc.

This is a work of fiction. Names, characters, places and incidents either are the product of the author's imagination or are used fictitiously, and any resemblance to any actual persons, living or dead, events, or locales is entirely coincidental.

This book was printed in the United States of America.

To order additional copies of this book, contact:
Xlibris Corporation
1-888-7-XLIBRIS
www.Xlibris.com
Orders@Xlibris.com

TO DANIEL STUART FRIEDMAN, MY HUSBAND.

ACKNOWLEDGMENTS

I owe thanks to many people: Sergeant Joe Haebe of the Santa Cruz Police Department; Dr. Mason, Santa Cruz County Coroner; the members of my writing group—Sharlya Gold, Erica Lann-Clark, and Bob O'Brien; to my former chef husband Malcolm for knowledge of a kitchen; and to author Laura Crum for the quote.

Many others have read and commented on the manuscript: my mom Vivian Hansen, my sister and brother-in-law Carol and Al Vogan, Nanci Adams, and my fellow murder mystery writer Genny Obert. Thanks to Rich Cowan for the skull and crossbones, Kimiye Welch and Justin Owens for their on-going computer assistance, and Herb Jellinek for his careful proofreading.

CHAPTER ONE

"Carol," my mom always said, "be careful what you wish for. It might come true."

Head Chef Jean Alcee Fortier was a case in point. I'd wished him dead a dozen times, and I remembered the last time clearly. I'd stumbled into Archibald's at three thirty a.m. in a semi-somnolent state. Even after years of working as a baker at this swanky restaurant, I hadn't adjusted to the hours.

I entered the building from the loading dock, which was on the front of the building, but well-screened from the brick U where valets in maroon uniforms with gold braid would later hustle to park Mercedes and BMW's.

A sixty-watt bulb illuminated the time clock. This was one of Eldon's subtle manipulations, to make us squint, and therefore to focus, on what we were doing. People underestimated Eldon. That was his m.o. The bumbling, mild-mannered Clark Kent exterior hid a cunning kitchen manager. He disarmed by dithering. He created a sense of incompetence while all the hard evidence suggested otherwise. For one thing, he'd held onto his job in Santa Cruz, one of the most competitive towns in the world for eating establishments. Secondly, the kitchen made a profit for the conference center.

The hall lights were off, but I knew the place like my home. On the right was the Employees Dining Room (EDR), and on the left the employee restrooms and unisex locker room. The hallway deadended in a supply room, a swinging door into the kitchen at its left.

I was more asleep than usual. Chad had awakened me at midnight with a cough he'd recently developed. He'd been busy sleeping right through his nagging little harumphs, until I shook him awake.

"What cough?" Even half-asleep, he was a hunk. His blue green eyes gradually comprehended and glinted with annoyance. "You woke me up to tell me that?"

"You're keeping me awake."

"Go sleep on the couch."

"You go sleep on the couch," I retorted. "Why should I have to sleep on the couch when you're the one who's choosing to gradually commit suicide with cigarettes?"

"You wait until the next time you get a cold, Carol."

"Cold, my ass," I muttered while I jerked my pillow and the top blanket and retired to the living room. Chad's breathing galled me. Life was not fair. Just as his deep breaths lulled me like a fountain, a cough lodged in the middle, like a skip in a record.

I'd slept not at all, and entered the fluorescent glare of the locker room in a sleepwalking state. Not that many years ago, the female employees had changed clothes in the tiny restroom, while the male employees commanded the convenience of the locker room. Then this last bastion of chauvinism had been converted to a unisex facility with a screened section in each of the far corners. I didn't see our head chef Fortier at first, but he certainly had seen me, and had made no attempt to cover himself. More naked than Adam, he sat on a bench in front of the lockers.

I gasped.

"Thank you," he said, in a voice like black velvet and old whiskey. "I know I'm good-looking, but I don't inspire many gasps." He smiled, a wicked, relishing grin, his white teeth set off by olive skin. At 3:30 in the morning and stark naked, he looked impeccably groomed, his black, wavy hair recently barbered and brushed straight back. He stood, revealing the works, broad shoulders, washboard stomach, and a penis to match his ego.

"Excuse me," I said, backing out. I should have known decorum was a wasted effort.

"Hey, Carol, don't go. My linguini needs some salsa."

"Salsa on linguini?" I stammered. "Yuck."

I went outside to cool my anger. The asshole. Why did all the women flip over him? Given the image only now fading from my retina, that was a rhetorical question. I understood how his young, new girlfriend Delores mistook his low-life humor for charm, but how could mature women like Suzanne or Concepción take in-consideration as joie de vivre? With the right looks, I thought bitterly, a person could get away with murder.

On the loading dock, I faced the grounds of the conference center and inhaled the jasmine and eucalyptus-scented darkness. Archibald's was on a wooded hill, high above the fog-shrouded Santa Cruz. I enjoyed the serenity.

I wondered what the hell Fortier was doing here so early, although in truth, he often was the second person to arrive. I begrudgingly acknowledged that he was deserving of his position as Head Chef, and wondered if a sexual harassment complaint would cost me my job. I was also pissed because I'd been too startled to think of a snappy comeback.

As I paced the concrete dock, waiting for someone else to arrive, I had one of those momentary epiphanies where I understood com-pletely why my husband Chad smoked: the spark, the warmth, the comfort. Looking back, I suppose I waited out there getting chilled because I expected the next arrival to be my buddy and comforter, Buzz Fraser. Instead, I heard a motorcycle roar through the night. Unlike the rest of us who parked a half-mile away and stumbled to the kitchen, Patsy drove her Harley right up to the dumpster.

"Hey, kiddo, whatcha doing out here?" the disembodied voice said. Patsy wore black leather, and I couldn't see her, only the winking red reflector on her helmet.

"Oh," I said airily, "I'm contemplating how to kill a son-of-a-bitch."

Another thing my mom used to say was "hold your tongue." Needless to say, I never listened. As a matter of fact, when she said that, I'd stick out my tongue and grab it to prove that I was the impossible, incorrigible kid that she claimed. Little did I know that I was about to develop a keen appreciation for my mom's clichés.

CHAPTER TWO

Only a couple of weeks later, on a hot summer day, which in Santa Cruz meant in the eighties, Patsy, Suzanne and I had gotten together and laughed over beer as we hatched progressively nastier ways to kill Fortier.

I'd met my two co-workers at a sports bar with a big screen television to watch the first episode of Cruz'n Cuisine.

"A cooking show," the bartender had said as he thunked our beers on the counter. "This is a sports bar."

And what a stupid idea that was, I thought. People kept opening them because they were trendy and the places kept folding in a trend. No one seemed to grasp that Santa Cruz was not Cleveland or Detroit. Santa Cruz had no home team, no unifying mania, no fans who would sit in empty, freezing stadiums to watch away games on screens.

I hadn't thought coming here was a good idea. "Let's chug-a-lug and go to my house to watch," I suggested.

"But we'll miss the opening," Suzanne whined.

Patsy planted her combat boots on the railing of the bar and leaned over the dark wood into the bartender's squarish face. "I know what kind of bar it is." Patsy had a body that should have drawn an admiring glance; she participated in the Santa Cruz Body Building Classic, and jutting toward the young man were breasts one usually saw only in magazines. However, the bartender's eyes zipped to her shaved head with the poof of mauve curls at the front, the ears riddled with rings, the tattoo on her forearm, and the burn scars all kitchen workers have. Biceps popped below Patsy's black muscle shirt. These details distracted him.

"The Master Batters and I come here all the time." Patsy

added in a gruff, but reasonable voice, "If anyone comes in and wants sports, you can put on sports."

Patsy, the pastry chef, had worked at Archibald's for the last three years, and like me, was in her thirties, so we'd bonded in spite of our differences.

The man's dark eyes darted around the room. We were the only customers in the bar except for a man in his thirties with a conservative haircut and a tailored suit, an anomaly for Santa Cruz.

"Customers come first," Suzanne said sweetly.

Patsy and I shot her dirty looks, but as the bartender inspected her, he underwent a transformation. His shoulders dropped, his mouth relaxed, his eyes softened.

Suzanne looked like a cream puff, with golden, sun-kissed skin exposed by a sleeveless, flowered dress. Permed, frizzy blond hair was banded into the topping.

"KRUZ channel?" He rotated his shoulders which cranked the football-player neck from his open white collar.

"Thank you," Suzanne said. "I'll buy you a beer."

I guess this was what my mom meant when she said, "You can get more flies with honey than vinegar." My sassy reply had always been, "God, ma, who wants more flies?"

The bartender graciously agreed to let Suzanne buy him a Coke, and then, to his credit, he drank it at the other end of the bar as he leaned over a newspaper.

The program started at four. The title scrolled across the screen and then our sexist Head Chef Jean Fortier waved as bright music played and the camera zoomed in. Fortier wore what looked like a uniform from Archibald's: white smock and chef's hat. "What's Eldon gonna think of the uniform?" I wondered aloud. Eldon was a born bureaucrat, the kind who counted towels and uniforms. He would have counted beans had Archibald's served anything so humble. But then, if Eldon had his way, we soon might. He advocated ethnic-cuisine nights. If this is Tuesday, it must be Italian. He'd recently had me experiment with focaccia. This had nothing to do with an appreciation for diversity, and everything to do with overhead. We could put lasagna on the table for less money than prime rib, lobster thermidor and Dungeness crab. Since most people in Santa Cruz were not rich to begin with, and nearly everyone was worse off since the earthquake, we needed to "attract a broader base of clientele."

"Eldon probably supplied the uniform in exchange for a plug," Patsy said dismissively.

I had to agree. That sounded like Eldon. "Is this filmed in his own kitchen?"

"Yeah," Suzanne said with chagrin.

Suzanne was sweet, built like a Barbie doll, and had once dated Fortier, which may have qualified her as a "dumb blonde." But she wasn't. Under the spray of frizz, lively brown eyes checked out the world. Of all Fortier's formers, she'd been on the most equal footing. She had an AA in Culinary Arts and Hospitality from Cabrillo College and was anxious to move up the ladder. She'd used Fortier for advancement as much as he'd used her for sex. Ironically, it had been Suzanne's promotion to head of the garde manger that had opened the door for Eldon to hire the beautiful Delores Medina, Fortier's latest pursuit. According to kitchen lore, Fortier had once, long before my time, romanced Esperanza Medina, Delores' mother. The kitchen was like a Melrose Place. But Suzanne showed none of the ire of a woman scorned. She'd gotten what she wanted.

On the screen, Fortier flashed a brilliant mouthful of straight white teeth and modestly introduced himself as the King of Cuisine. "Everybody loves something sweet, dahlin'," he said, putting on his New Orleans accent. "Especially me." He winked.

"The pig," Patsy muttered.

No one in the kitchen hated Fortier more. A lesbian and a radical feminist, Patsy loathed womanizers. Fortier ranked right up with Rush Limbaugh.

The man in the gray, pin-striped suit watched the program from his table. The bartender looked up worriedly from the sports section, but the guy didn't make any indication he'd rather see baseball.

"Today I'll show you how to whip up a special delicacy—oeufs a la neige," our gorgeous Jean Alcee Fortier continued. I could imagine women around the county, tuning in, vibrators in hand. He could whip up tuna salad for all they cared. "Don't worry, the preparation of oeufs a la neige is easier than the pronunciation." He had all his ingredients and equipment assembled on the counter and turned a careful profile to the camera as he poured milk into a chicken fryer.

"If Buzz had gotten the show, that could be you up there, Patsy," I murmured, even as I wondered if that were true. Would a local station air someone as radical looking as Patsy? My heart felt a tug and ache for Buzz Fraser. He was hands down my favorite person at work. He rubbed aloe on my burns and told me Chad was a lucky man. This television program should have been his, and he'd been eager to share the limelight. He'd proposed that I appear to make breads and Suzanne guest star to prepare salads. As I thought back to when Fortier had magically usurped Buzz's program, bubbles of anger zipped to the surface like water about to boil.

"Hey, bartender," Patsy called aggressively.

He raised his head from the newspaper.

"Got any darts?"

He ignored her, looking back at the sheets spread on the counter.

Fortier spelled the name of the dessert, a rather nice touch, I thought, in spite of my anger.

"Another name is floating island because we'll create little islands of meringue in a delectable custard. In N' Awlins, we make this as a birthday treat."

"I bet he'll be able to sell his cookbook now," Suzanne said.

Patsy and I exchanged blank looks over her golden head. Neither of us had known anything about a cookbook. Because Chef

Fortier behaved stupidly, it was easy to forget that he was talented and capable.

"Why did you want to watch him on big screen?" Suzanne taunted Patsy, insinuating that even she might be vulnerable to his charms.

"He wouldn't fit on a little one," Patsy snorted.

"Poor Buzz," I said. "I wonder if he's watching."

"Why torture himself?" Patsy chugged the last of her Red Hook as Fortier separated eggs with expertise. "If I were Buzz, I'd kill the asshole."

"Yeah," Suzanne said dreamily, eyes still on the screen, stripping Fortier to his full glory, as I'd seen him two weeks earlier.

The memory of the locker room incident fueled my anger. Later that day, Fortier had backed me into a corner of the kitchen and breathed into my ear, "A little too much for you?"

"Why," I'd whispered back, "does a guy with a gorgeous, nineteen-year-old girlfriend who should assuage the worst of mid-life crises need to harass a thirty-something, married woman?"

The word "harass" backed him off about an inch. He smirked, raised a perfect, thick eyebrow, and stretched one arm to the wall. Even in a chef's jacket, even in a kitchen where no colognes were allowed, even with my anger, there was no denying his musky masculinity. He exuded pheromones like a skunk.

I slugged him in the bread basket.

Fortier emitted a satisfying grunt and dropped the arm. "Ow, chingado," Victor, the dishwasher said. He dropped a huge, stainless steel bowl on the tile.

As the bowl spun and rang, I slithered past Fortier. "Huh," he sneered, "if you thought for a second about sexual harassment, you can forget it." He grabbed my sleeve and pulled me back to his body as the embarrassed Victor picked up the bowl. "You even think about telling Eldon, and I'll get you for assault. I have a witness, and you don't," he hissed.

Suzanne nudged my shoulder and brought me back to the reality of the sports bar. "Buzz should make some preserves and not quite cook 'em enough," Suzanne said jokingly. "If he left them in the kitchen, the King of Cuisine would taste them sooner or later." It was a strain for Suzanne to be so "bad," but she wanted to fit in with the crowd.

"Sooner," Patsy said. Fortier was famous for sampling and critiquing.

"Botulism is not a reliable vehicle."

They both turned and stared at me.

"Even if you canned sloppily, you wouldn't be guaranteed botulism, and there's no way of knowing whether you've produced it or not, short of testing the stuff on your cat."

The bartender, who'd slid down the counter to check on us, kept a slight distance and listened. It wasn't botulism, but me that fascinated them, much as a squished bug might.

"Don't you know murder is my hobby?"

"Tell us the best way to do it. How would *you* kill Fortier?" Patsy smirked as she rubbed together her hands and cut her eyes toward the bartender, still hoping to make him wary.

Beyond Patsy's shoulder, the suited man raptly watched the program, extracting a black leather organizer and a gold pen from his jacket.

For a moment I imagined using Fortier's head as a volleyball, but Patsy hadn't asked for the most satisfying method, she'd asked for the "best." I assumed that meant a successful way that would avoid detection. "Poison." I was a lightweight drinker and felt buzzed as I started my second beer. "Sure, take Empress Wu, who rose from a concubine to be the only female leader in the history of China. She strangled one baby and had some rivals' hands and feet chopped off, but mostly she used poison. Before she became empress, if her husband so much as looked at another woman, the woman had a way of dying after dinner, didn't matter if it was her sister or her daughter."

My audience had lost interest in the program. Three sets of eyes gazed at me. I hardly ever had a chance to hold forth on my favorite topic, so I continued, a little disappointed that I hadn't snared the interest of the suited man.

"Then there's Agrippina, who killed Claudius, by feeding him a mushroom from her plate. Or, for a serious alchemist, take the Marquise de Brinvilliers. She tested her stuff on children in a charity hospital."

"That's awful," Suzanne interjected.

"Well, she must have perfected the art, because when she went to nurse her ill father, she slowly poisoned him to death, and he was so unaware of the connection that he thanked her for her care with his dying breath."

"Gives me the willies," Suzanne said. She pulled a pink scrunchie from her hair, shook the blond frizz down and then pulled the spray up and rebanded it, so it looked more or less as it had before.

"Oh," Patsy rejoined, "you ever seen *I, Claudius*?" I could tell this was gang-up-to-gross-out Suzanne, a common kitchen pastime. "I can understand why Agrippina killed that idiot." Her strong face took on a meditative look. "Murder was probably one of the only ways women could gain power in those oppressive times."

"Well," I said, "going back to the original question, given the overworked state of the police and the burden of proving guilt beyond a reasonable doubt, it's easier to get away with murder than books or movies would have you believe. Especially if you use poison and plan."

"Sorry to interrupt."

Patsy and Suzanne jumped, but I'd seen Mr. Slick moving toward us. What he lacked in height, he made up for with tailoring. The suit was well-cut and he looked like money down to his supple, Italian loafers.

"I noticed that you seem to know this chef." Dark, all-business eyes flicked at the screen. "He's very good. He's a natural in front of the camera, and with his looks and that accent, he'll make the female audience swoon."

Patsy and I exchanged a look of amusement since neither of us was in need of smelling salts.

"Who are you?" Patsy asked.

From the leather organizer he slipped out a card and plunked it on the counter. His name was less important than the curly black words: Exploration Channel, Programming Acquisition and Development.

CHAPTER THREE

Before trying to drive, Suzanne, Patsy and I walked to the nearby Carpo's to put food in our stomachs. Carpo's was a crowded, noisy family restaurant featuring some of the best fries anywhere and slabs of homemade pie.

I called Chad to let him know I'd go from the restaurant to my volleyball class. I kept shorts, my old athletic shoes, and knee pads in my car. Signs of an addict.

"I hope you don't plan to go poking your nose into Fortier's business," Chad said bluntly.

His irritation suggested he'd spent time after work hauling around his mother. "I beg your pardon." I slathered on the indignation to make sure he heard it over the background clatter of trays. Still, I understood Chad's insinuation. Depending on who a person asked, I was nosy or curious, stubborn or persistent.

"Have you been drinking?" Chad asked.

"Only two beers."

"I hope you aren't driving."

"Not at the moment."

Chad sighed in exasperation.

I didn't think drinking and driving was a joking matter, either, but my husband's protectiveness annoyed me.

"Are you sure you should go to volleyball?"

After reassuring Chad, I went to join Patsy and Suzanne. They'd reached the front of the line and had drawn the eyes of every man who could look without craning from a booth or getting socked by his wife. It didn't hurt when I joined them. Thick, auburn hair sprayed down, accenting my strong, five-foot-eight build. I wasn't as cute as Suzanne or as striking as Patsy, but I could hold my own somewhere in the middle ground.

The three of us spent an hour eating, speculating about Mr. Slick's business card and what it could mean for Fortier, lamenting that the opportunity hadn't befallen Buzz.

"But if it were Buzz," Suzanne said, "the guy might not have been interested. He specifically mentioned Jean's sex appeal."

"Don't you think Buzz is sexy?" I asked, nibbling the end of a substantial fry and challenging the two women across the table.

Patsy's muscled arms moved into an elaborate, palms up, Greek shrug and the dragon on her bicep moved, shooting out its flame. "Sexy? Penises are the most ridiculous-looking things in the world. How can anything so obvious be the least bit erotic?"

"There's more to men than their penises," I snapped. Patsy's male-bashing could get tiring.

"Tell them that." She took another big bite of burger. In spite of all her effort to look like a self-proclaimed "dyke," Patsy's creamy, oval face remained unconvincingly doe-like.

I skewered Suzanne with my eyes. She stopped mid forkful of salad and squirmed in the vinyl booth. "What?"

While an innocuous blue green, my eyes had fire in them like an opal. Or, like a crazed maniac's. "Do *you* think Buzz is sexy?" I suspected Suzanne had shifted her affection to my friend, although Buzz didn't believe it. Working around Fortier had obliterated Buzz's sense of his own sex appeal.

"A little," Suzanne hedged. She put down her fork and rearranged her hair. "Not like Jean."

"Thank God," Patsy muttered. She used both hands to pick up her burger, and let a trickle of juice run down her forearm. "Fortier's an asshole." She stretched her mouth so wide that I could see the fillings in her back molars. She took a bite, chewed it a little, and talked around the food. "How can an asshole be sexy?"

"Do either of you know how Fortier got that show instead of Buzz?" I asked, steering the conversation away from Patsy's diatribe, wondering, not for the first time, what had made her so bitter.

They both shrugged. In spite of the warmth generated by all the people and the steaming food in the open kitchen, Suzanne's fragile shoulders looked like they could use a sweater. The summer evenings cooled fast with incoming fog. "Geez, I thought if anybody would know, it would be you," she said.

"When I've asked about it, Buzz mutters and says Fortier is an asshole."

"See," Patsy crowed. "Buzz agrees with me."

"Everybody agrees with you," I snapped. Then I felt bad. Suzanne had dated Fortier, after all. And while we all pretended that she'd dumped him after receiving her promotion, she was too nice to have done that. In truth, Fortier had already decided to chase after young Delores Medina. While Fortier had been Suzanne's paramour, the kitchen workers had begrudingly noticed his good points, but his play for Delores had solidified his position as Major Asshole. Still, our constant ragging about Fortier indirectly criticized Suzanne.

"Being an asshole runs in the family," Patsy said. "I hate Fortier's little twit niece, too."

"Alexis?" I hardly knew the girl because she worked the afternoon shift, but Patsy had to deal with her as part of the pastry department.

"She's sweet," Suzanne protested. She wielded her fork like a hockey stick and moved a kidney bean puck down the expanse of her plate.

"If you don't mind room temperature I.Q.'s." Patsy wiped her face and threw a wadded napkin on to the center of the table. "Uncle Jean this, and Uncle Jean that," Patsy mimicked. "She acts like Fortier's a fuckin' god. She's been in pastry like four months and the other day she starts telling me how to improve my mousse."

"You said yourself that she's parroting Fortier," I said in my most pacifying voice. Patsy in a full-scale rant was not a pretty sight.

"No doubt," Pasy agreed. "People are idiots." She rose from the booth. "Present company excepted," she muttered and then smiled.

Later, as I drove my '66 Karmann Ghia to volleyball class, I combed through everything Buzz had said about the cooking show, which took about one minute. The couple of times I'd broached the subject, he'd given me a clear message that he didn't want to talk about it.

I drove past Gayle's bakery which held no temptation for me. I spent five mornings a week with my nose encrusted with flour, invaded by the smells of sour dough baguettes, apple muffins, and snickerdoodles. The aroma from the bakery simply reminded me of work, and watching the cooking show had stirred up old questions. Chad's comment about my nosiness held something akin to foresight.

I parked in the nearly full lot of the New Brighton Middle School gym, and climbed out into the chilly mist. How had Fortier usurped Buzz's show? I planned to find out.

My mother used to call me Carol Cat; she also frequently reminded me that curiosity killed the cat. The admonishment had done nothing to deter me, and I was fully alive at last report.

As I approached the double door, a pack of middle-aged yuppies and gym rats in shorts and sweats, their faces and hair damp, were leaving the gym. I entered the comforting embrace of sweat and dust and reverberating noise.

CHAPTER FOUR

Five months later, when Patsy grabbed Head Chef Jean Alcee Fortier's raven hair and hoisted his dead face from my lebkuchen dough, I uncharitably thought the man had remained a pain in the ass to the end.

Fortier's body fell heavily against Patsy. A spontaneous crowd of kitchen workers jammed the hallway outside my bakery niche. Patsy and the new, back-line cook Todd lowered Fortier from the stainless steel table to the tiled floor near the dishwashers.

Eldon waddled like a prodded duck to the hall phone to call 911.

"Is he breathing?" asked Delores Medina. Tears welled in her blue eyes. Esperanza, her mother, stood behind Delores with a hand on either shoulder.

"Pobrecita," she soothed. Esperanza tried to turn her daughter to her breast, but the girl stared, transfixed, at the man on the floor.

Todd skillfully pressed two fingers to Jean Alcee Fortier's carotid artery. "I don't feel anything. Can anyone here help me with C.P.R.?"

"Yo," said Patsy. In her chef's uniform, she could be mistaken for a regular person. She pushed back Fortier's chin, probed his mouth with her fingers, and breathed into the already rubbery-looking body while Todd worked his chest like bread dough.

The sight of Patsy putting her lips to the bloodless ones of Fortier was nearly as astonishing as his yellow, apparently dead body.

Eldon returned from the phone and grumped. "What was he

doing here? He was supposed to go home sick. This is just what we need, for a known chef to die in our kitchen. How is that going to look?"

"El Punetero," Victor muttered. Everyone but Eldon knew he'd been called The Masturbator, but no one smiled.

"He's breathing!" Delores cried.

"No, mija," Esperanza said. "Tha's Pad-zee's breath causing the movemen'."

Eldon fluttered nervously at the perimeter of the group. He patted his hands. "Come on, you guys. Everyone but Patsy and Todd, back to your stations. We have a kitchen to run." Eldon was the only one among us who could manage a kitchen with a dead man on the floor. I guessed that was how a six-foot-two dumpling became an executive chef: Buzz was a better cook, Fortier had been more flamboyant, and everyone was better looking.

We dispersed reluctantly. I heard the sirens shrieking up the wooded hill from the hospital, a convenient mile away.

"Oh, good Jesus, sirens," Eldon moaned. He puttered nervously to the back line where Ray had returned to work. He lifted the lid of the lunch soup du jour—vichyssoise—that Todd had been preparing. He ladled up a sample, blew on it, and delicately slurped.

"Todd still needs to season it," Ray said.

"I can tell," Eldon commented dryly.

I stepped around the body, back to my table, and looked at the huge pan of brown, spicy dough for the lebkuchen, a Christmas honey cake that I baked as individual cookies. Earlier, Fortier had pulled the mini stepladder that floated around the kitchen over to my work area. He must have been sick. It was unlike Fortier to sit. I wondered if he'd been sampling my dough. It would be like him to taste it and then die, his final act designed to find fault. His apparent death disconcerted me, but I didn't feel sad. The kitchen was like a family and his death was like losing a relative one didn't like. I felt the loss, but not any grief.

My lack of compassion made me feel less than human, which increased my churlish mood.

I'd even missed the climactic moment, having been on the other side of the kitchen in the pastry department, helping Esperanza Medina unload a huge bottom tier for a wedding cake.

The body stretched behind my compact work area toward where Victor and his second cousin Abundio washed dishes. They were speaking low, rapid-fire Spanish. The only words I picked out were la chota and La Migra. The death had them worried about who might show.

When the paramedics arrived, I turned to watch, but Abundio slipped out the door to the Vista Dining Room and Victor kept his thick, square back to the excitement. They acted like the INS were imminent. I hadn't thought much before about the routine fear of their lives. No one in the kitchen would rat on them, not even Eldon with his "This is America; speak English" attitude.

The two paramedics looked like they doubled as lifeguards. "Good job," one said. Todd and Patsy stood, stretched, and rubbed their joints. One of the paramedics hooked Fortier's body to a respirator, and the other exclaimed, "Whoa, I know this dude. He's that famous cook."

He was right, but no one in the kitchen responded. I glanced at Buzz, but like everyone else, he was acting as if he hadn't heard the paramedic's comment. Like everyone, he was acting as if there weren't a dead body in our midst. For the last five months as I'd prodded and pried, Buzz had kept the same stoic, stony countenance in response to the cooking show.

I looked again at the stiff, quiet workers. Maybe the kitchen crew had convinced themselves the inert mass could be revived. I knew Fortier was dead. I turned back to the vague shape of Fortier's head pressed into my lebkuchen. The dark dough was still cold from its night in the refrigerator. I baked it.

CHAPTER FIVE

Archibald's perched atop eighty acres of eucalyptus and redwoods and the back windows commanded a view across Santa Cruz to the Monterey Bay. In 1929, the Society of Mary (Marianists) had constructed the long, elegant, two-story main building to serve as a boys' high school. It now housed meeting rooms and the restaurant. Shortly after the arrival of the paramedics, the police had tromped through the main entrance, below an arching facade once crowned with a cross.

In pleated uniforms, the police strode through the main lobby, down the hallway to Vista Dining Room and then into the kitchen. Eldon was in a dither. Why couldn't they have entered from the loading dock and side entrance like the paramedics?

"Good Jesus, what will our customers think?" He wrung his hands as he gave the officers a piece of his mind.

The two policemen collected names and basic where, what, when information. One left briefly, and not more than twenty minutes later, two detectives in plain clothes arrived. This did not bode well. The appearance of detectives meant the paramedics had been unable to jump start Fortier.

The female detective, a woman of Junoesque proportions, waved to Patsy. Patsy's smock and chef's hat hid her mauve curls, tattoo, and muscle definition. I was surprised an acquaintance would recognize her so easily; she looked normal if one could say that about any of us in our houndstooth pants.

Although Eldon had a couple of inches, and many pounds, over the detective, the woman treated him like a gnat, slightly annoying, but hardly a presence with which to reckon. She introduced herself to him as Detective Peters. In spite of her ordinary gray slacks, ivory blouse, and charcoal blazer, everything about her bearing blared cop.

Her partner was younger and more casual, dressed in Levi's, dress shirt and tie. He had a smooth, kind face, not yet world weary or jaded. A crooked nose added the right touch of toughness. He looked like one who'd become a cop out of civic duty or because his father had been one. He didn't look the anal-retentive, steroid-using, power-tripping type. Standing under the mistletoe Fortier had taped to the ceiling only yesterday, he introduced himself to Eldon as Detective Carman and they shook hands.

With pads of paper in their hands, the uniformed officers stood in the middle of the kitchen and read back the information they'd collected to the detectives.

"Buzz?" the female asked.

One of the officers pointed and Buzz turned, holding a small knife. He'd been cutting fresh sage from the kitchen's herb garden and the kitchen was redolent with its pungent fragrance. "It's on my driver's license," he said stubbornly.

When Buzz decided not to talk about something, it was useless to pry. I'd learned that as I'd tried to find out about the television program Fortier had stolen.

The detective seemed to sense this. She glanced warily at the knife and her eyes scanned the room, noting knives everywhere.

The detectives asked the officers a few questions as we all listened, slack-jawed and transfixed, even as we automatically performed our tasks. I stood at the door of the bakery so I could see all the action. The detectives dismissed the officers.

Eldon guided them toward me. "There are three ways into the kitchen from the dock," he said, hinting that the police should use one of them. "There's a door near the walk-in refrigerators, and, if you go through this swinging door into the hallway, there's a door at the end. There's also a door into the EDR. The Employees' Dining Room."

The two nodded respectfully, but their eyes were already roving into the bakery, down the metal racks, over my body. Peters, the female detective, turned around, took two long strides to Victor's area, peered into the chute to the abyss of the dishwasher's garbage disposal, inspected Victor and the tray he'd loaded for the conveyor ride through the washer, and touched the swinging straps at the other end. "Looks like a mini-car-wash," she muttered. Peters glanced at the Styrofoam cooler under Victor's counter. "What's that for?" Oddly, I'd wondered that a hundred times, but for all my native curiosity, had never asked.

Victor studiously ignored Peters, pulling into himself, his compact body dwarfed by the detective.

She persisted, asking if he'd seen the incident.

"No entiendo."

Her male partner surprised everyone by asking the question in flawless Spanish.

Victor said he hadn't seen anything.

Eldon gave his rendition of events, and bounded off to make sure no one's brunch would suffer just because Fortier had the bad taste to die in the kitchen.

Detective Peters turned to me. "Fortier collapsed into dough?"

She and Detective Carman both looked over my shoulders at the five rows of six cookies on each of ten sheets. Detective Carman had the graciousness to breathe in the spicy air, but the female detective simply looked alarmed.

"Want one?" I asked cheerfully. "Right out of the oven."

Detective Peters looked at me as though I were a smart ass. "You destroyed evidence?" She had sandy hair, almost as close-cropped as Carman's. I wondered if she had a temper. My mom always associated the highlights in my auburn hair with my temper.

"Evidence of what?"

She didn't want to answer that question. For all my interest in murder, I only then realized Fortier might have been killed. I'd thought the detectives had come simply because the death was weird. Suspicious. The thought of actual murder, right where I was standing, lit in my gut and struggled to my brain.

"Were you here when it happened?" she asked me.

"The murder?"

She scowled. "No one's used that word."

"No, I wasn't here when *it* happened. I was over in pastry."

She gave me another one of those looks that said we weren't hitting it off, and turned back to the main kitchen. She diagrammed the area and snagged Eldon long enough to confirm the names and phone numbers the uniformed cops had gathered. Detective Carman photographed.

"Do you have anyone who *saw* anything?" Detective Peters asked Eldon, with a hint of weary sarcasm.

"Patsy was over here. She'd brought some bowls for Victor and Abundio to wash." Eldon wrinkled his fleshy forehead, and looked around, his mouth in a moue. Abundio was not at the dishwashing station.

Detective Peters strode across the kitchen behind the lead line and back line chefs to the pastry department and returned talking amiably with Patsy. Perhaps because Patsy's uniform covered her shaved head and tattoos, or perhaps because the female detective seemed attracted to her, I was struck by Patsy's prettiness, the widely-spaced green eyes animated by their interaction.

"So what was this guy Fortier doing when he collapsed?" Detective Peters brusquely switched to business as she and Patsy reached the bakery.

Both detectives kept using that word, as though they didn't even want to say he died until it was official, the relatives contacted, the notice in the paper.

"He was sitting on those steps. He was holding his stomach and he looked like he had the flu." Patsy gestured toward the steps, folded and set aside in the hall, and then toward the stainless steel table that occupied most of the bakery. "He was sampling Carol's dough."

Both detectives glanced toward the brown, spicy cookies cooling on my counter.

"He didn't die from my lebkuchen," I said defensively. I picked up a cookie and bit into it.

"Are you all right?" Detective Peters exclaimed as she watched my face.

"Ah shit!" I said.

Since I wasn't dying, her interest waned. "What's wrong?"

"I forgot the citron."

"Well I don't think that's what made Fortier sick," Patsy said, "even if he was a perfectionist. He was like the expression green around the gills. I couldn't believe he was eating."

That did seem implausible, but why else would he be in the bakery? "Maybe he was so sick that he sat on the stool to rest." Fortier usually didn't sit in order to sample; he was more the dive-bombing type.

Patsy reared back. Sprigs of mauve hair popped from her chef's hat. "He had a finger in your dough," she said hotly.

"Ladies," Eldon murmured.

Patsy turned searing eyes to our large, soft manager. Her muscular frame pumped, growing larger like a mating frog's, her preface to holding forth, probably on the disgusting baggage of a word like "ladies."

Detective Carmen took one tentative step into my domain and Patsy noisily exhaled.

"Jean . . . ehm, that's Mr. Fortier, did say he was sick and going home," Eldon said, trying to gain control. "I asked if he wanted me to call a cab."

I felt claustrophobic with two representatives of the law, Patsy and Eldon boxing me into the nook.

"So what was he doing here?" Detective Peters asked.

Eldon shrugged.

"He could never stay out of the kitchen," I said.

I guess they heard the resentment in my voice.

Detective Peters scratched one sandy eyebrow.

"He was always tasting and adding spices and suggesting. He was a pain in the ass," I blurted. It felt refreshing to say that and not worry it'd get back to Jean and my job would be at stake. His near celebrity status had given him more power than the title Head Chef merited.

"Maybe he left and returned to drop off his Kris Kringle gift," Eldon suggested.

"Fortier," I scoffed. "I can't believe he participated."

"He got a present this morning," Eldon said stubbornly. "A jar of honey."

"If he actually left, it's most likely he came back to see Delores," said Patsy.

"That's Delores Medina," Detective Peters said, checking her notes.

"Right-o."

Patsy led the troop back across the kitchen, turning left before the pastry area, into the garde manger's domain. There the lovely Dorothy Medina worked under the tutelage of the completely different, but equally lovely Suzanne Anderson, turning out salads of bulgar wheat with apricots and dates, mixed greens and spinach, and melons cut into baskets overflowing with crudités.

I could breathe again.

CHAPTER SIX

I caught my dear Chad on the back steps smoking a Camel. He started and quickly stubbed out the cigarette on a potted cyclamen. As much as I adored his James Dean looks, I was adamantly opposed to this detail. Even though the Christmas season told me to be giving, and even though I had exciting news, I unleashed a sarcastic, "That doesn't look or smell like a Vantage."

"It's another type," he said slyly. He stroked Lola, our brindle cat, who rested on a lawn chair. She stretched her front legs and yawned.

"And I know exactly what type." I unpinned my braid and untwisted the ropes of chestnut hair.

"Christ, Carol, I spent all morning on a slippery roof in the fog. I need to relax."

"Take a nap." In spite of my tongue, Chad admired the loosened mane. As a kid, I'd hated the wild, thick hair. Now I considered it one of my best features.

"You have no appreciation for how dangerous my job is."

After seeing Fortier dead, less than an hour ago, this remark didn't sit well with me. "As dangerous as it might be, it's not as dangerous as that thing you had in your mouth. I'm willing to bet more smokers die of cancer than roofers of falls."

He stood and stretched. He was gorgeous. Round buns in 501's, brown, brawny arms exposed by a tee-shirt in spite of the December chill. "Well, hello and good afternoon to you, too." There might have been a wee bit of sarcasm, but basically Chad was easygoing. He meant to change the mood.

"That's it," I said angrily. "If you aren't going to take quitting seriously, I'm buying that life insurance."

I harrumphed through the sliding glass door and stalked into the tiny second bedroom in our tiny house, located in the sunny banana belt of Santa Cruz. In this sanctuary, I kept my collection of murder mysteries, true crime stories, detective books, and references on guns and poisons. The first three were fine with Chad, but the last spooked him. There was a practice range up in the hills past Archibald's and I'd once hinted that I'd like a gun for target practice. Chad had been appalled.

I riffled through hanging file folders for the insurance proposals to prove *I* was serious about this matter.

Chad leaned in the doorway and watched me silently with blue-green eyes like my own, giving me time to think about how he'd moved his smoking to outdoors, how he'd reduced the quantity, and had switched (for the most part) from Camels to lower tar and nicotine brands. He'd tried Nicorette and even, occasionally, listened to the subliminal messages on the tape I'd bought him.

"I'm trying, Carol."

What more could a person ask? Only a foolish woman would have persisted with a wavy-haired hunk making such an earnest plea. I was she.

"You're only thirty-five and you already have a terrible cough, Chad."

He was looking sadly at my ringless left hand. If I wore my ring to work, I had a doughy mess at the end of the shift, but Chad didn't seem to understand that. He looked hurt when I forgot to put it back on, as though, without it, I'd be carted off at the end of the day by some womanizer like Fortier.

"How much would you get?" Chad asked.

"A hundred thousand is a standard sort of minimum policy."

He allowed a pregnant pause, and then asked, "Where's that book?" His eyes roamed over my battered desk, and along my book shelves.

He must have meant my latest acquisition, a reference book that I'd taken to work to browse during break and to shock people.

"*Deadly Doses?*" I rhetorically asked Chad. "That's in my locker, at work, where, incidentally, Jean Alcee Fortier died this morning."

It wasn't the smoothest segue, but now I was ready to change the mood. Then the mournful look in Chad's eyes clicked into place. The poor guy was entertaining the notion that I could have another motive for wanting an insurance policy. The idea struck me as funny and I laughed.

"I don't see anything funny about someone dying." He looked so unsettled that I laughed harder, lost all my annoyance, and tackled him.

"It's not funny," I agreed.

"Then why are you laughing?"

"You . . . ," I managed between hysterical gasps. But, that wasn't it either. The truth was that I may have disliked Fortier, but his death, his possible murder, upset me, and I'd been twisted tight all morning and now I was popping loose.

Chad looked stunned as though he thought the maniac sitting on his stomach intended to dispatch him on the spot.

I took a deep breath to still myself and managed to coo, "It'd be much too incriminating to kill you here."

Besides, in spite of my volleyball legs and the arms I'd developed from hefting huge bowls and trays of dough, I couldn't overpower Chad. He quickly remembered that and we wrestled and made up on the Turkish rug. Lola sauntered in to watch this curiosity.

My mood felt significantly improved after we made love on the floor. Chad's defensiveness melted away into my arms. We kissed tenderly, a peace offering as we separated. The phone rang.

"Would you get it?" Chad asked, heading for the bathroom, still naked from the waist down.

Still half naked myself, I lifted the receiver. "Hello." I'd never mastered a chirp. I always sounded like someone who hated to answer the phone, which I was.

My greeting wasn't answered. "Hello," I said again. "Bueno," I tried in case the person spoke only Spanish and were frozen with dread. Then another thought occurred to me. "Mary? Hello, Mary?"

"Isn't Chad there?"

She hated it when I answered the phone. She was the type of mother who preferred to pretend her son was single.

"He's indisposed."

I could feel her freeze over the phone. "Well, I guess I'll have to take the bus to go shopping," the long suffering voice began.

"You could call back in five minutes."

"Oh, no, I know he has a busy schedule . . . ."

I zoned out. If she really acknowledged Chad had another life, she wouldn't have called in the first place. I was happy that she wrapped up her self-pity and we said our goodbyes before the toilet flushed.

Chad could deal with the call as he wished. I needed to find Esperanza a Christmas present. This was the nineteenth and beyond Esperanza's little Kringle gifts, I'd done no shopping. Besides, I needed to get a sympathy card for Alexis, Fortier's niece who worked second shift.

After taking a shower, I donned fresh jeans and my Jose Cuervo Volleyball Tournament sweatshirt. Although I didn't play much beach doubles volleyball, I enjoyed watching the event each year.

I drove my Karmann Ghia to Way of Life. I loved my poor man's Porsche even though the exterior was rust red, the interior smelled like dusty oil, and the whole contraption rattled. Tucked behind a health food store, Way of Life featured gallon jars of herbs, natural cosmetic items like lotions, a wall devoted to books on herbal, homeopathic, and folk cures, and close, freestanding shelves crammed with gift items. A heady mix of fragrances greeted me at the door.

Since nearly two hundred people worked at Archibald's, we Kringled within departments and shifts. I had drawn Esperanza's name from Buzz's chef hat. We were surreptitiously to deliver recipes, little gifts, and snacks to our person until Christmas Day. The day after Christmas, when our seasonal push had ended, we'd have our party and exchange the slightly bigger gifts. For now, these were heaped in the upstairs lounge under a fir decorated conservatively with red balls and tinsel. I felt guilty that I hadn't yet added to the colorful pile, not that Esperanza would care. She wasn't like Suzanne, who shook or poked a package every time she passed the tree.

At the end of one set of shelves, I pawed through a small woven basket of earrings. I tried to imagine some amethyst crystals dangling from Esperanza's ears, but there was something too delicate about them for her. She was a tough lady. Once she'd accidentally burned a strip across four fingers that had raised into a path of marble-sized blisters. She'd iced them and finished her shift.

Not that she looked weathered. Delores Medina, Fortier's last girlfriend, had clearly gotten her looks from her mom Esperanza. They looked more like sisters than mother and daughter. Esperanza was petite, with flawless olive skin, and long, thick black hair just beginning to gray. If the gossip were to be believed, she'd been Fortier's first conquest in the kitchen.

Admiring blown glass vases, I turned the corner and spotted my mother-in-law entering the store. If I'd been in Woolworth's, I wouldn't have been surprised and I would have had an opportunity to evade her.

"Carol," she said, as startled as I was.

To my excruciating embarrassment, I realized she was probably shopping for my gift. After years of unworn polyester robes, recycled silk flowers, and unused smelly perfumes, Mary still had no clue what I'd like, but at least she knew more hopeful spots to fish.

"How'd ja get here, Mary?"

"The bus. I can't bother Chad every time I want a ride across town. I know you young folks need time to yourself and I don't want to interfere in your lives." She patted her maroon hair, pursed her red lips, and tugged her tight, short, nubby yellow jacket over her huge stomach.

She, in fact, called Chad every day.

If I mentioned it, Chad cringed and said, "Carol, she's seventy-two."

"Oh," I said in mock surprise, "she told me that she was sixty-two."

Chad shrugged patiently. "Lots of people, especially older people, lie about their ages."

His mom lied about everything.

"We should be glad she's as independent as she is."

"You'd think if she wants to pass for sixty-two, that she'd act more like sixty-two," I muttered.

I resented that Mary had never been independent enough to learn to drive or to cut the umbilical cord, unlike my mom, who was also widowed, and a year older, my mom, who'd commented years ago, "Carol, why do you always pick men with mothers?"

Our conversation ground to an awkward silence. I dutifully offered, "I need to find a gift for my Kris Kringle at work."

"Well, honey, I have no idea what young people like."

The tone sounded sympathetic. Yet, I knew she meant we young people, anyone under forty, were difficult and picky.

"You know I'll be working Christmas Eve and Christmas Day," I said, in case she harbored any illusion of a family celebration. I tested the fabric of a small rug between thumb and forefinger.

A customer squeezed around Mary's girth. Mary didn't move. "I don't understand people going out to eat on holidays." She puckered her mouth and in spite of her withered face, managed to look like a baby. "It lacks tradition."

"Brunch or dinner at Archibald's is their tradition."

Another customer entered and detoured to a side aisle. "You like that rug, honey?"

"Mmmm. Great texture," I said, "but it's light. Slippery." I moved closer to the shelves. "Look at this." I held up a small brass menorah with seven white candles to lure her from the center of the aisle. Before she could criticize the item, I said, "I'm sure I'll get overtime both days, especially now Fortier is dead."

"The Cruz'n Cuisine King is dead?"

Since the Exploration cable channel had picked up the program, Fortier had become a minor celebrity. Women may not
have swooned, but they adored his sleek, French good looks, his
exaggerated New Orleans accent, and his San Francisco Culinary
Academy training. His cookbook was not only being published,
but also plugged for free on every program.

I stood in one place, fingering objects, afraid to move with
Mary in tow. Besides, of all the aisles, this was the widest. I told
her about Fortier's collapse.

"Poisoned," she said with the conviction of a gypsy looking
into a crystal ball. "He was poisoned."

CHAPTER SEVEN

The Fortier family managed to arrange a funeral in three days. With Christmas looming, and Fortier's pertinent parts sent to Sacramento for analysis, there was no reason to keep the family in limbo. As busy as Archibald's was, a solid contingent from work attended the service. Even Eldon slid hurriedly into a pew. Officer Peters had been there, too, scanning the chapel full of suspects. She didn't question anyone. Perhaps she was waiting for someone to throw himself over the open coffin and confess.

Suzanne wanted to attend the burial, so I rode with her to Collins Rolling Acres Memorial Park. Fortier was laid to rest where we'd drive by him every day. The graveyard sat across the street from the hospital, providing a cheerful view for patients. The hospital had recently added a residential facility and terminally ill customers could travel in a convenient circuit from hospital to housing to grave, a route my brother Donald could have used.

I liked Collins Rolling Acres. The cemetery lacked the manicured green of places like Forest Lawns, suburbia for dead people. Here, after five years of water conservation in response to the drought, only hardy grass survived. Even in fifty-degree December chill, the place had charm. The markers dated back a hundred years, old enough to be historically interesting, yet none of them was ostentatious or pretentious. I wished Donald had chosen a plot here so that I'd have a solid place to mourn him.

The priest intoned the lovely "earth to earth, ashes to ashes, dust to dust, in sure and certain hope of the resurrection onto eternal life." As Fortier's casket was lowered into the raw new hole, my heart ached for my brother, his ashes floating, or dissolved, in the salty sea out from Ft. Bragg. My poor mom, the victim of a cosmic mix-up. First she'd had Donald; then she'd had me. Since Donald didn't "come out" until his twenties, I may have been the harder of the two. To hear my mom, I first refused to get born, but when I finally plopped on to the delivery table, I asked for cowboy boots and a gun. God had definitely gotten her orders scrambled. I'd once heard someone ask my mom about grandchildren, to which she'd dryly responded, "My children don't reproduce."

Those who wanted stepped forward to toss clods of earth on the casket. I liked the hollow thud, the note of finality. The reminder of our fragile, precarious state filled me with needed humility. I wished Donald had chosen this ceremony instead of cremation.

As we dispersed from the pit, Suzanne fell in step beside me. She dabbed at the corner of an eye.

I gave her a brief, sideways hug. "You okay?"

"He had his good points," she snuffled. Dressed in black, stirruped stretch pants and a mid-thigh black cashmere sweater, she looked pale and lovely.

"Of course."

She looked at me suspiciously, although I'd meant to concede the point graciously. I'd never met a pure swine or angel. People were complicated. I had only to look at my small family. On one hand, while Donald had promiscuously used sex to make a point, my mother referred to him as a "bachelor," even as he was dying of AIDS.

"Hey," Suzanne said, "your eyes are teary."

I nodded in acknowledgment.

She sighed and her body relaxed. "Jean was generous, fun to be with, and great in bed," Suzanne testified.

"I'm sure he was." I hoped my tone sounded comforting. Given Fortier's success with women, I'd assumed the latter. I also had no trouble believing that when he took out a woman, he wined her and dined her in a slow-paced luxury that blinded her to the inevitable conclusion.

Suzanne's brown eyes peered incredulously into my damp ones. "Hey," she said, "did you . . . . Did Jean . . . ?"

"Oh, no." I suppressed a giggle. "Me?" I stuck out my puny chest. "Look. Now if Fortier had been a leg man . . . . Nah, he only liked me for my scintillating personality." I tried to imagine Suzanne crazed with jealousy, concocting a poisonous brew to kill Fortier. But even aided by Suzanne's black clothes and currently somber mood, I couldn't imagine her as a murderess. In theory, I believed everyone capable of murder. I certainly was. Yet, I told myself that if Suzanne had killed Fortier, it could only have been by accident. I realized fully that I believed Fortier had been murdered, that Mary was right about the method, and that I was damned interested in finding out who done it.

"Who was that with Alexis?" Suzanne asked, brightening.

I smiled grimly, and looked up the knoll to see if I could spot Fortier's diminutive niece, although I knew who Suzanne was talking about. I was surprised she hadn't already gotten the scoop on Alexis's companion. Suzanne was losing her touch. "That's Fortier's ex from New Orleans."

"I didn't know he'd been married."

"Me neither."

Suzanne's yellow bug was parked in a lane that curved around the low hill. Suzanne perched on the wheel well of her car and diddled with the black ruffle in her hair.

"Good thing we both have skinny butts," I said, bumping her to create room for me. Behind us, near the groundskeeper's house, the lines of the flag pole dinged in the crisp air. I looked off toward the wooded hills leading to Archibald's while Suzanne lit a clove cigarette.

Suzanne exhaled pungent smoke. "So how did you find out about Fortier's ex?"

Other mourners trickled down to their cars. Alexis and the mystery woman left the grave with a man who had to be Fortier's brother—Alexis' father—and the tiny, white-haired mom, her old face red with silent weeping.

"Eldon. He called Alexis when Fortier . . . died." I didn't feel ready to share my suspicions. "This woman answered and said she was Julieanne Fortier. When Eldon heard the name, he thought it more appropriate to tell her the news than to leave a message for Alexis, but first he decided he should know who she was."

"She's not what I'd expect," Suzanne whispered as the four black figures approached. In deference, she ground the cigarette against the tire, put the unsmoked portion in a small, enameled case, and tucked it in her black clutch bag.

"Except for the tits, me either," I whispered back. The inside of Fortier's locker at work left no doubt about his fascination with large, mammary glands. Julieanne was plain with shoulder length, brown curled hair. Her body was not fat, but lacked muscle tone. From years of observing naked women at the Spa, I knew how she'd look undressed, her stomach, butt and spreading thighs dimpled with cellulite, her ponderous breasts losing the fight against gravity.

"What is she doing in Santa Cruz?" Suzanne asked.

I slowly replied, "That's what I plan to find out."

CHAPTER EIGHT

When I opened the door, Chad was wrapping a large box in red foil. He labored in the middle of the oak floor.

"For me?" I asked coyly, putting hands over my eyes. Through the peek holes, I spotted his mom at the end of the couch, planted like a Buddha. I grimaced at her, all playfulness vanishing. I disliked this woman from the maroon hair down to the duck feet crammed into shoes that she pretended fit because they'd been on sale. In a week, she'd want Chad to haul her to the podiatrist. Compared to the roiling I felt in Mary's presence, my past reactions to Fortier seemed like sardonic amusement.

"Hello, Carol," Mary said in a voice that might fool Chad as he wasn't looking at her. The small eyes pinned me with loathsome jealousy that declared I'd never fully appreciate this gift. "We couldn't find any scissors for the paper."

(No "How was the funeral?") "You couldn't find the scissors, Chad?" I wasn't having any of her "we" shit. At *her* house scissors would have been easily located, not because she was organized, but because she had four or five pairs.

Chad shrugged. "No problem. I just tore it. You're gonna love this present, Carol." He beamed.

"Don't tell me what it is." I hastily departed to our bedroom. I couldn't watch Chad wrap; we wrapped to different drummers and Chad dropped hints while I liked surprises. I'd have to work to keep this present a secret, even with only two measly days until Christmas. I also wanted to get away from Mary and change out of my black skirt and heels into some sweat pants.

On the nightstand I kept my one photo of Donald, his senior picture. I picked up the heavy, pewter frame. He looked clean-cut, handsome, athletic and straight, as he no doubt yearned to be. What could be more painful than being a homosexual teenager? I turned the plastic latches on the back, popped out the cardboard, and removed the paper from behind the photograph. I'd cut it from the program for his service. One thing about dying slowly, you could plan your funeral. Donald had chosen this passage from Lewis Thomas' *The Lives of a Cell*: "The obituary pages tell us of the news that we are dying away while the birth announcements in finer print, off at the side of the page, inform us of our replacements, but we get no grasp from this of the enormity of the scale. There are 3 billion of us on the earth and all 3 billion must be dead, on a schedule, within this lifetime. The vast mortality, involving something over 50 million of us each year, takes place in relative secrecy . . . ."

I guess that put death in perspective, I thought, as I returned the clipping to its spot, but it made me feel so gloomy that I returned to the living room. Chad was putting the Scotch tape into a kitchen drawer.

"I got a great deal," Chad said. He held the package (about as big as a bread box) against his plaid flannel shirt. Tape prodigiously bandaged the bright red.

Chad's mention of a "deal," filled me with fear. Possibly this was the beginning of his evolution into a person like Mary, a person whose life was ruled by the word "sale." Although Mary lived on Social Security, I'd known her to buy ten chickens at Safeway because they were on sale. Of course, she'd had no where to freeze them, so that had meant an instant party. Barbecue was the easiest, but she didn't have a grill. But we did, and our patio . . . . I feared Chad would become Mary, just as I feared that I'd fall into my mother's world of cliché. Even hating my mother-in-law seemed like cliché.

"Wanna feel how heavy it is?" Chad asked.

"Nah, that's okay, Chad." I didn't need to touch it to guess he'd bought a C.D. player. We'd discussed the idea several times.

He lowered the gift to beside our potted tree that we'd hauled in from the back yard. The box dwarfed it.

"I feel bad, Chad. I don't even have an idea for your present. Unless you want a plot at Collins Rolling Acres Memorial Park. At the funeral, I thought it would be a nice place to be buried."

Mary fanned herself with a scrap of wrapping paper. "Thinking about such stuff at your age isn't natural. Now, when you are old and decrepit like me, that's a different story."

In some ways my hatred of Mary was unfair as she couldn't focus on me long enough to hate me back with the same intensity.

"When I was your age, ..."

She stopped, trying to remember either what my age was, or what she was doing back then.

Normally, Chad would have started a peace-keeping campaign by now, but he seemed disconcerted by my remark. He wrinkled his forehead. "Boy that funeral put you in a cheery mood."

I forgave his sarcasm. If I'd spent the afternoon with his mom, I'd be way beyond cutting remarks. He was probably miffed, too, that I hadn't paid proper attention to his gift.

His mother smiled smugly, happy at the hint of dissension. The simper didn't even unwrinkle her lips.

"Mary said Fortier was poisoned." His inflection seemed to add, "And where is that poison book of yours." This was silly. Maybe Chad thought I could be a cold-blooded killer, that I had knocked off Fortier, an idea no doubt encouraged by Mary, who probably smirked at a secret vision of me behind bars. "Geez, Chad, I'm not going to slip hemlock into your eggnog." I peered in the refrigerator for a snack. "At least, not until you're fully insured." I couldn't help myself; my perversity had attacked. I turned and watched with satisfaction as Mary's lips dried into prunes. The down side was the small jolt, like a muscle spasm, in Chad's neck.

"Do the police have any suspects in the Cuisine King's murder?" The timing of her question and her emphasis on the last word dripped with unpleasant implication. She sniffed, her lips puckered.

"Detective Peters attended the service," I said airily, "but they haven't even declared Fortier's death a homicide."

"Channel 8 called it a suspicious death," Chad said. He was sweeping up the scraps of paper and ribbon from his wrapping job.

I felt piqued that I'd missed the television coverage. Eldon had done a great job of suppressing the news. The *Sentinel* article had been small, vague, and second-page.

"Let me do that, honey." Mary struggled from the couch, making an elaborate show of reaching for the broom, in spite of her poor, swollen feet.

"Sit down, Mary," Chad commanded.

"You need some help, son."

"I don't need any help."

"This murder is just the gruesome thing to interest Carol," Mary said, settling her large rump back on to the cushions.

My neck prickled with antagonism. "I do think it's more stimulating than a sale at Mervyn's."

Mary's thin eyebrows shot up, but she wore a tight smile.

Chad sighed in exasperation as he emptied the dustpan. "You better watch out that Carol doesn't start playing detective," she warned Chad.

"Hello, Mary." I pranced in front of her, crossing my arms like semaphores. "Yo, over here." I was regressing quickly, and I hated her for it. "I am in the room."

"Well, I know you are, dear," she said in a saccharine voice, smug with victory. She'd reduced me to a twelve-year-old right before my husband's eyes. "I'm telling my son this because I don't think he knows."

"Knows what?"

She heavily blinked her stubby, painted lashes like it should be obvious what she meant. That was the flash point. I burned to my scalp. Chad didn't need to worry that I might investigate a murder; he needed to worry that I'd commit one. "If I decided to *play* detective," I spit into the wrinkled face, "I'd be damned good at it."

She smiled with condescending patience, secure in the protection of her son.

Chad decided to whisk Mary away from his half-crazed wife, across town to a one-bedroom HUD apartment near the railroad tracks. As soon as they roared off in his Ford truck, the mail came. Lola followed me out to the old-fashioned metal box on a post. My calm slowly returned. "Let's see if you won that cat food sweepstakes."

She meowed in agreement and looked up expectantly.

Inside the box were some junk mail fliers and a letter from a screen writer, a distant friend. I'd written him in a flurry of excitement about an idea for a movie: a woman collects a cool million in insurance money after she knocks off her drunken husband by plastering his chest with Habitrol patches. My distant friend politely thanked me, and then asked a barrage of questions about the story that indicated he found the plot a bit implausible.

"Have you ever thought you might be in the wrong line of work?" he'd written. "I just can't imagine you braiding dough. You should be a private investigator, a forensic pathologist, a reporter on the city desk, or maybe a mortician."

I hugged the European-style writing paper to my heart. Someone who believed in me!

Lola protested: "Open the door, my pompous, silly person." She meowed indignantly. "I thought I'd trained you better than this."

I turned the knob and entered my resolve. I'd bury Chad's mom without killing her. She'd rue the day she'd made that quip about my being a detective.

CHAPTER NINE

The next day after work, I sat glumly at the indoor fountain at the Capitola Mall. The water had been turned off and the circle converted to a Christmas wonderland. I detested the mall, especially the day before Christmas. The hordes. The masses. The mind-numbing joviality. My chest tightened, the way it had many moons ago at rock concerts, but now it wasn't from eau de marijuana. What if something excited the crowd? A fire? An earthquake? A blue light special? A person could be trampled.

The mall reminded me of the plant in *Little Shop of Horrors*; it fed on people and grew and grew. The growth had exceeded the ability of the life lines to support it. Coming from the south at this busy time, one waited through four or five changes of the light to exit the freeway to 41st Avenue. Then the traffic moved sluggishly like blood through a clogged artery.

I looked around for local television crews who roamed malls to humiliate last minute shoppers.

I'd considered buying Chad a C.D. case containing several choice discs, maybe even a best of Van Halen that would be just for him. But Chad didn't know how obvious he was and I didn't want to enlighten him.

I needed something for my mom, too. Her gift to me would be crocheted, possibly useful, but just as likely to be an orange toaster cover.

What to buy for Chad and how to investigate Fortier's murder, bumped and mixed with piped-in Christmas carols and the tidal hum of hundreds of frantic shoppers. I sat at the edge of the waterless fountain and dug my hand into a box of caramel popcorn. I liked snacks that I could grind between my teeth and that I didn't see at Archibald's.

The police were investigating the "suspicious death," but the tox screen would be done in Sacramento and it could take weeks before they could officially declare the death a homicide.

The kitchen staff seemed determined to believe that Fortier had suddenly been gripped by a massive coronary. But, for once in my life, I agreed with Mary. The quick, deadly flu-like symptoms Eldon reported suggested poison. I couldn't understand how someone like Mary, who had the sensitivity of a whetstone, could have intuition as sharp as a fillet knife. Yesterday when Chad had returned from taking her home, he'd said worriedly, "Mary thinks you're going to get tangled up in this."

"I'd make a good detective," I'd grumbled, rankled that a friend, distant both emotionally and physically, could recognize that, but Chad couldn't.

"That may be so, but you're not a detective."

He was right, but I felt like he was siding with Mary. "I could be like Rat Dog."

"Rat Dog?"

"Don't worry. She doesn't have a gun. She just tracks down dirty rats."

"She's real?"

"Shit yeah," I'd said, pissed off by Mary's phony concern, that now had Chad worried. Without a doubt, the woman intended to undermine me, but she was so disorganized and inconsistent with her attacks, I could never formulate an effective defense.

Even now, after cooling off for twenty-four hours, I felt irritated as I replayed the scene. I bit into an old maid, shooting pain up my jaw and temple. I tried discreetly to pick the ground seed from a molar, but with my short nails, I had to abandon delicacy. Naturally, I then spotted the blond, suited, female reporter with her mike and the man behind her with a video camera. Fortunately, they missed my excavation and honed in on a big, frantic-looking man in the corridor. I looked again. Eldon.

He was the last person I wanted to see, but I wondered what inspired him to frenzied shopping. I decided to tail him. He ducked into a jewelry store, as though evading the press, afraid perhaps they'd ask his place of employment and then, from there, about Fortier's death. For a simple evasion, Eldon was going to extremes. He'd confronted a weary-looking clerk, and had begun such a self-absorbed monologue that I entered the store behind him with no fear of detection. The slender, clean-cut clerk, who looked as though he'd rather be anywhere else, set a velvet tray on the glass counter.

"Yes, something along these lines," Eldon said. "She has brown eyes, so I think gold findings would look better than silver, don't you?" The young man opened his mouth, but Eldon continued. "Delicate, not clunky."

The clerk silently lifted a pair.

"More feminine."

The clerk glanced hopefully past Eldon at me, so I edged out the open entrance and melted into the flow headed toward Sears.

To me everyone in the kitchen was now a suspect, so I considered Eldon for a moment. He was the fussy, methodical kind who might use a poison, but why would he knock off Fortier, who'd added prestige to his kitchen?

Poison was a rare way to kill. According to my books, it accounted for about one half of a percent of homicides. However, poison was also a smart way to kill, and I imagined people got away with it which skewed the statistics. What I couldn't understand was why anyone, poisoned and sick, would stop in the bakery to eat lebkuchen dough.

Sears' furniture section spread to my right. I plopped into a cozy, tweedy armchair and tried to imagine Eldon with a woman, someone for whom he'd buy earrings. From the chair's safety and in the hypnotized state malls induced in me, I gazed at shoppers. In the past, when I'd wanted to know more about crime, I had pestered both the coroner and Sergeant Gold of Homicide. Both had impatiently tolerated me on the phone, probably because they didn't know how to hang up on a woman. I'd never met either man. For all I knew, they could be among the frenetic shoppers.

To investigate, I'd have to question everyone from the morning kitchen shift. That task would be formidable even if people cooperated, and even if I didn't count the waitpeople who moved between the kitchen and dining rooms; Big Red, the cook in the employees' dining room; or the housekeeping staff who picked up dirty towels and uniforms and delivered fresh ones.

Besides, for all the excellent motivations in the kitchen, weren't these things usually domestic? And, poison seemed like a woman's method. Of course, that same reasoning could point to his lovers in the kitchen. He'd worked his way through the women as though searching for an answer by process of elimination—Esperanza, Suzanne, Delores and God knew who else. I had to start somewhere, and even though she wasn't employed in the kitchen, the ex-wife seemed as good a place as any. To find out about her, I needed to talk to Alexis.

No time like the present, even if it were a cliché, Christmas Eve, and the day after the funeral when Alexis probably had not only Julieanne, but also her father and grandmother staying with her.

With an effort, I lifted myself from my warm nest. The swarm had thinned, but I dodged the remaining, desperate shoppers, who hurtled from store to store like juggernauts. At the entrance, I called Alexis at Archibald's. She couldn't see me that night, or on Christmas, but she still planned to go to our employees' party the day after, and promised to talk to me then.

I escaped the mall, drove across the street to Cymbaline Records, purchased a handsome oak CD holder and several discs— Springsteen, Hungarian Rhapsodies, Garth Brooks, and Poi Dog Pondering. I'd wrap each CD separately, disguising the shapes to create suspense, and more presents, for Chad. I meandered down to the Capitola Book Cafe and bought my mom a book. I could wrap at leisure, as Chad had taken his mom to Mass and would dine at her apartment. Now that I'd solved my shopping problems, I had only a murder case to solve.

CHAPTER TEN

Baking on Christmas Day was horrible, not because I was sentimental and minded working on the holiday, but because I had to crank out fourteen hundred pieces—stars and apple strudel and cranberry Danish pockets from puff pastry; Danishes with raspberry jelly and jalapeño jelly, and sugar cookies in Christmas shapes.

As I twisted dough, I sifted through the usual motives for murder—love, money and revenge. Revenge suggested Buzz. Love? Well, that got complicated fast. Money? I had trouble grasping money as a motive. It didn't seem like there could ever be *enough*. Not for murder.

I hated raw dough, but I pulled a little piece from my finger and nibbled it, trying to remember if I'd put in the vanilla. Normally I liked my day to be busy. "Idle hands make the devil's playground," had been instilled in me from youth, but today my mind wandered farther afield than automatic pilot. The nibble made me suspicious.

"Carol, want to see me walk on my hands?" Victor asked. He was Esperanza's brother and Delores's uncle, but had a whole other set of genes. His flat, Indian face more striking than handsome, he grinned at me from the door.

I pinched a marble of dough and thrust it at his face.

"First taste this."

It was a routine command, and he ate from my finger with closed eyes and exaggerated smacking. "Tase like . . . ," he smacked some more, ". . . Tase like dough. Gringo food. No tase."

"Does it need salt?"

He pinched another sample from the mound on my table and

repeated the charade. "No."

"All right. Let me see you walk on your hands."

He made a show of wiping his hands on one of my white towels as though preparing for a cartwheel. Then he stooped and placed his foot on one hand, then the other.

I smiled.

"Good joke, huh?"

"Great joke."

He turned to go. Tasting and joking were the depth of our relationship.

"Victor, how much money would it take for you to kill someone?"

He straightened to his full height which was about five foot eight because his offended eyes stared right into mine. "Me kill someone?"

"A hypothetical situation," I said, and added, "pretend."

"If I didn't like the cabron, if he raped my sister or something, I'd do it for free," he said. "But I wouldn't kill someone I liked." He scratched his dark hair thoughtfully. "Not for a million dollars." In Spanish he bade me a good day and spun on his heels.

Well Victor felt as I did, but I knew that people did kill for money, sometimes piddly sums if they were desperate. With his recent successes, Fortier could have a nice nest egg. One person might know about Fortier's financial affairs, but it wasn't going to be easy to extract any information from Concepción Galisanao.

Not even a former employee of the year escaped Christmas duty, but then Concepción rivaled Eldon for company loyalty. Down the hall in personnel, the tiny Filipina had been at Archibald's since its opening ten years ago, which given the hospitality business's turnover, made her an institution. Concepción was the Head of Human Resources. She sat primly at her desk, reading over half glasses. She'd adored Fortier, not because she was fooled, but because she felt it was nice that he bothered to flirt with someone her age.

I extended two cellophane-wrapped brownies.

"Oh, Carol, my favorite!" She smiled up at me, wagging a finger back and forth in the air, the nail manicured and painted with a minuscule wreath. "But no time off."

I held onto the brownies. A person would never surmise from the woman's figure that Concepción lived on a candy bar diet—one delicious Hershey's for breakfast, another for lunch, and a wholesome, satisfying Symphony bar for dinner.

She fanned herself with the papers she'd been considering. "Too hot for Christmas," she said in her accented, helpless voice that made people forget that she was ruthlessly competent.

I wondered if the ageless Concepción Galisanao could be having a hot flash. Her office felt cool to me. But then, I'd been in the bakery all morning. Any place would seem cool to me. I sat opposite her. She wore a red dress; candy cane earrings peeped from her dark hair. From this distance, she could smell the brownies, made with pieces of Belgium chocolate. I played with the cellophane to make sure.

"No time off for anyone until we hire someone." She smiled. "No time off forever." A ring-bedecked hand with a Christmas decoration painted on each nail crept toward the brownies.

"Fortier's death was tragic." I lifted the brownies from the desk.

She gave me a tight smile and one, slow blink of her eyes. "Does that mean you didn't kill him?"

Concepción was impervious to bullshit which was why everyone liked her.

"So you think he was murdered, too?"

She shrugged. "That's for the police to decide." The sibilance slurred with saliva. She smiled. Concepción Galisanao could smile as she scheduled you for sixty hours. "Maybe you say it's tragic because no time off."

"No, I think it's tragic because someone killed him. I want to know who."

"One of the women in the kitchen," Concepción declared.

"Maybe. I intend to find out."

Her chocoholic's eyes, transfixed on the two brownies, misted.

"I heard Fortier got a big raise after his program took off."

"Everybody heard that."

"Well?"

"Ten thousand dollars."

"Whew!"

"Not really whew when you consider our wages," Concepción staunchly defended.

"How about the beneficiary of his insurance policy, Concepción?"

"I can't do that," she quickly replied.

I peeled the cellophane from a brownie. "I know. Employee confidentiality. But Fortier's dead."

"Are you going to eat that damned thing?" Concepción snapped.

"I brought them for you."

"Then let me have them, Carol." The little woman lunged for the brownies.

I jerked them away. "Careful, Concepción," I said indignantly, "you're going to smush them, and these are ultra fudge masterpieces with hunks of walnut in them. Crispy outside and chewy centers."

Concepción crossed her arms. "I can get some from the kitchen."

I smiled smugly. "No you can't."

Concepción crossed the small office to a file cabinet and found the hanging folder. "Jean upped the standard work policy to twenty thousand and the beneficiary is . . . ." She turned to me with her nose wrinkled, "His wife?"

"Ex-wife," I corrected.

"Says here 'wife.'"

I looked over her shoulder. Under beneficiary it said in Fortier's scribble: Julieanne Fortier—wife.

I handed Concepción the brownies. "Thanks. You've been a big help."

CHAPTER ELEVEN

Christmas night was not a success. I did my best to act surprised as I ripped open my big present from Chad, but I'd never been a gifted actress. My lack of oohs and ahs translated in Chad's mind as disappointment. Plus, Christmas reminded him that I didn't attend church, that I was, as his mother put it, "a heathen." Chad fell into a melancholy funk.

Now as I crossed the mauve carpet of Archibald's lobby, through murmurs of my colleague's conversation, I hoped this day-after-Christmas party proved more fun. I looked forward to buttonholing my colleagues. Fortier's niece Alexis didn't have any button holes in her black velvet frock, but I seized her tiny wrist and towed her to the balcony. She didn't know me that well, but she didn't protest. "Whadzup?" she asked in typical twenty-something banter. Her nearly black eyes looked annoyed, but curious.

Out on the balcony, I released the young woman's arm. The fog swirled up the hill, obscuring any view and dampening our faces. At last year's party, several employees, drunk on champagne, had leapt from the balcony to the lawn below. Big Red had broken his leg. This year the party was sans alcohol and subdued. There'd been many such changes in the last year. After a series of prime rib and steak thefts, Eldon had had padlocks installed on the walk-in refrigerators, and since February art was displayed only in the halls and not in the lobby as someone had sauntered out the front entrance with a small watercolor piece.

I hadn't thrown on my coat and the chill penetrated my long-sleeved, turtleneck dress. "Forget your coat, catch a cold," my mom would say, like that bumper sticker: Play an accordion, go to jail. That's the law.

"I'm sorry about your uncle," I said to Alexis.

"Yeah, right." Her petite frame diffused in the foggy night, but I heard the spite, and sensed, more than saw, Alexis pull herself to her full five feet.

"He was an excellent chef and my heart goes out to you."

"You guys all hated him!" The apparition flounced by to the rail. She was young enough to get away with that kind of behavior. "Probably one of you killed him. Like that bitch Patsy!"

I followed cautiously, as though sneaking up on a finch, tiny, flitting, with a voice like ungreased machinery. "Patsy?" I prompted.

"You know how some women are when they can't get what they want."

I nearly laughed. Patsy *want* Fortier? But maybe she knew something I didn't. At least she wasn't in denial about the murder like the rest of the kitchen.

I hadn't known what to expect. I saw Alexis only occasionally as she ate in the EDR before her shift. That was after my shift, when I took advantage of the free food, our nicest fringe benefit.

As I leaned on the balcony rail, she jumped away from me. "He was eating your batter!" she charged.

Dough, I mentally corrected. Alexis looked like Fortier with strong Gallic features, dark hair and eyes. They were simply less dashing on her; Fortier's appeal had depended heavily on charismatic energy.

"Yeah, I don't understand that part," I grumbled, "but I agree he was killed."

Her eyes grew to the size of quarters, as though she'd made the accusation without meaning it. "I can understand why you guys didn't like him," Alexis continued tearfully, "but as an uncle, he was great. Generous. He got me this job, you know?"

"I know." I straightened and touched the luxurious softness of a black velvet cape thrown around her dress. She was the second person to mention Fortier's generosity. He'd lived in a condo near the yacht harbor. The way California property values had skyrocketed before the plateau of the current recession, his condo could contain a hundred thousand dollars worth of equity. Then there was the money from Exploration's acquisition of the cooking program and the cookbook he had in the works. Now he was dead, would his wife Julieanne profit from his generosity? At the funeral, she'd looked a little down in the heel.

"I'm surprised you had Jean's ex-wife come stay with you," I said.

"Julieanne?" she asked. "I don't think they divorced." She didn't sound sure. "Besides, she's my godmother. Jean was my godfather. Neither of them had any kids, and they competed for me. Especially after my mom left." She sighed. "I liked the attention and money and stuff, but it was kind of exhausting."

"Are your dad and grandmother still here?"

"No. Julieanne drove them to the airport so I could come to the party." She sounded worried. "I should have done it."

"Why?"

She chose not to answer.

"If Jean and Julieanne are separated, what brought Julieanne to Santa Cruz?" I asked, trying to sound nonchalant. I rubbed the goosebumps on my arms and pulled down the sleeves that I'd push up in another minute, a habit from years of working in dough and aggravated by sleeves that were always too short.

"I like to think she came here because of me," Alexis said. She took a tissue from the pocket of her cape. "But she came here because of Jean. They split up fifteen years ago, and she's still not over him." She delicately blew her nose. "I guess she'll *have to* get over him now."

"What did she do in Santa Cruz?"

Alexis's eyes narrowed. "Why are you asking me all this stuff?"

"Because I think the same thing you do. I think he was murdered."

"So why do you give a shit?" Her eyes flicked me up and down.

"Were you one of his girlfriends?" she asked contemptuously.

I shook my head. "Not his type." That was true, but it made me feel pissed off at Fortier even though he was dead. Because I so clearly wasn't his type, there was no mistaking his harassment for anything else.

Alexis smiled sardonically, but in spite of her hostility, she didn't walk off. She wanted to talk. I stared silently into the mist, as though hoping for a sign that Santa Cruz existed.

"Julieanne worked at KRUZ t.v. as a secretary."

I felt like saying something dumb like, "Holy cow," or "No kidding?" No wonder Alexis acted as if she were making a confession. The information held all kinds of implications. I didn't want to ask my next question. I felt as though I'd already taken advantage of Alexis's vulnerability. I was lucky; I didn't have to.

"I'm sure she helped Jean steal Buzz's show," Alexis grimly volunteered.

CHAPTER TWELVE

Alexis assumed the morning crew's silence on Jean's theft indicated ignorance. Tact, like rumaki and caviar canapes, was a taste appreciated and understood with age. She informed me that Buzz had planned the Cruz'n Cuisine show. "Everything, even the title, was his idea." She wheeled and pronounced, "I'm too cold out here."

I followed as she pushed through one set of French doors into the heart of the party. Tables of elaborate hors d'oeuvres had been set up opposite the Christmas tree. Boiled shrimp piled on a bowl of ice, garnished with lemons. I wondered if I'd have a chance to eat, as I planned to do some serious mingling.

"So how'd Julieanne get KRUZ to switch to your uncle?" I asked Alexis.

People milled, crowded the plush mauve chairs and couches, and nibbled shrimp with mango sauce between sips of sparkling apple juice. Eldon, dressed as Santa Claus, stood behind the food table. As we passed, he handed each of us a paper plate with a petit four. "The pink one's for Alexis," he said. "My own creations."

Alexis led me away from the crowd into the wide hallway to Vista Dining Room. A few people sprinkled the hallway, admiring the art display, probably recorded by discreet cameras. A couple sat on one of the austere, dark blue settees, holding hands and speaking demurely. Alexis eyed my plate. "I'd rather have chocolate frosting."

"Here. I'll trade with you." Her petit four was topped with a sugary rose. I didn't care which I had since my work had numbed my appetite for sweets.

"Julieanne kept Jean posted on Buzz's progress," Alexis softly continued our conversation. She nibbled a bit of cake with her front teeth like a rabbit. She may have preferred chocolate, but she obviously wasn't a chocoholic like Concepción. "Buzz made his pitch and the producer liked the idea. That's when . . .

Alexis froze. Then she abruptly turned to the wall as though enraptured by the watercolors on display. Walking towards us from the Vista Dining Room were Suzanne Anderson and Buzz Fraser.

Suzanne looked cold in an electric blue dress that scalloped over her breasts and ended well before the knees. The tiny bolero jacket looked like scant comfort.

She walked arm in arm with Buzz, but I doubted they had a date. Suzanne liked to flirt, and Buzz was tirelessly accommodating.

"Hi, guys," I hailed. Alexis whirled toward me, her face red, her dark eyes resentful and full of terror.

"I have to go to the restroom," she blurted, and clipped back toward the lounge as fast as her spike heels would allow.

"What's eating Alexis?" Suzanne asked. She removed the blue band from her hair and slipped the elasticized ruffles around her wrist.

I shook my head, although I had an idea.

Buzz Fraser watched the long, dark hair billowing behind Alexis. The young woman slowed only to toss her unfinished petit four in the garbage. I tried to read Buzz's expression, but he was noted for his unflappable nature in a work place where people had monumental egos, given the relative insignificance of their jobs. His look might have been one of concern or mere curiosity, but he did watch her until she disappeared into the restroom. Then he gave me a hug. Buzz wore soft brown cords and a warm, woolen sweater in a swirl of mellow earth tones. Even in the brief embrace, he felt snuggly. He smelled like eggnog, although I hadn't seen any at the party.

"Where's Chad?" he asked.

"When he learned there wouldn't be any booze, he refused to be dragged. Spouses need alcohol to make these things bearable."

This wasn't true. Chad liked to talk to people, but given my intention to snoop, I hadn't encouraged him to come. He'd been a little hurt and suspicious.

"Are you just going to admire that cake?" Suzanne asked.

I held the poinsettia-designed paper plate aloft and cast a critical eye on the petit four's rose. "Why not? It's Eldon's objet d' art."

Suzanne frowned. "Eldon might say that, but the flower is pure Patsy."

"Since Chad isn't here, I'll expect you to dance with me," Buzz said.

"You bet."

Like Fortier, Buzz wasn't conventionally handsome. High, prominent cheekbones recessed and dominated his blue eyes. Powder fine, blond hair puffed away from his scalp. Yet, a force of personality, polar to Fortier's, rendered him handsome. Buzz possessed an unpretentious calm.

I wanted to do more than dance with Buzz Fraser.

CHAPTER THIRTEEN

Back in the lounge, the tall, jolly Santa Claus bumbled a tiny green package. Buzz got us each a coffee and I perched on the arm of a couch, with my elbow on his shoulder. Suzanne leaned on the back of Abundio's chair. He looked back at her, blushed, and squirmed with pleasure.

"This is Christmasy," Buzz whispered, touching the ends of my scarf.

I'd tied it around my shoulders at the last minute for the Christmas colors in the pattern of bright red roses and green leaves on a gold background. It was like Buzz to notice exactly what a person wanted noticed.

My loose hair spread down over my shoulders and Buzz touched it, the way a person might sample a fabric between fingers. He was the only man who could tempt me from Chad, probably because he was too honorable to try it.

I set aside my paper cup of coffee, but didn't want to abandon the petit four where Eldon might see it. The coffee was a special blend with a hazelnut flavor, but I liked coffee black and unadulterated, as I preferred unadorned vanilla ice cream. A bit of a purist, I guess. I liked the individual tastes of things. I sampled the pink flower with my finger. It was pure. Pure sugar.

The employees sat haphazardly on the window sills, couches, chairs and thick carpet. On the outer rim of the circle some leaned against the wall. Eldon was in his element—center stage, in-charge, promoting the company. He was a born bureaucrat and must have been miserable as a cook, before he worked his way up to head of the kitchen.

He called for the fourth time, "Alexis?"

People didn't bother to look around. They wanted Eldon to get on with it. He reluctantly returned the package to the still large pile below the tree.

I wasn't going to learn any more about Alexis's godmother aunt this evening. Buzz didn't ask what had happened to Alexis. Buzz, ever the perceptive one, must have noticed his effect on her.

Eldon picked up a red foil box, all tape hidden, a lavish white bow on top. While I'd never buy a dress or shoes or a household item with bows, they looked good to me on presents.

"This is for Esperanza," Eldon hammed.

I leaned down and whispered in Buzz's ear. "Let's sneak out to the balcony."

"Don't you want to see what Esperanza got?" he teased.

"Glow in the dark Band-Aids, aloe vera cream for burns, and a spatula so she can quit borrowing mine."

He arched one pale eyebrow.

"I have a black sense of humor."

He smiled, a rare phenomenon that transformed the severe Scottish features. "I don't know. That's what Esperanza would like."

There he went again. Saying exactly what I wanted. Reassuring.

"She's a pretty earthy lady," he added. He held the door for me as others jealously noted our escape. "Even if she did have that thing with Fortier."

Cold fog enveloped us. Buzz hugged me sideways into the warmth of his sweater and I almost dropped the petit four. We walked to the rail and peered into the nothingness.

"When did they have their fling, anyway? It was before my time."

"Except for me, Fortier and Esperanza, it was before everybody's time."

"Before Eldon's?"

"Oh, yeah. Fifteen years ago, at least. I have to give Esperanza credit, though. She's the only lady I know who ever dumped him."

This was astounding news to me. "What happened?"

"If I remember right, she had a husband who suddenly resurfaced."

"You know I think Fortier was murdered?"

"Yeah," he whispered, as though we were having a romantic conversation. "You know, this thing Fortier had with Delores is more complicated than people think."

"How so?"

"Esperanza broke his heart. I really think he was in love with her."

"So Delores was a revenge?"

He shrugged and spread wide the fingers of his free hand. "Maybe it was a silly attempt to recapture the love."

My baker's nose again detected eggnog. With rum. "I want to figure out who killed him," I confided.

"Be careful, Carol. Nobody likes people poking into their business, least of all a murderer." The warning sounded harsh, unlike Buzz, but, on the other hand, when had we ever had occasion to discuss a real murder. He released my shoulder and wove his large fingers around a strand of my springy hair. "Once a person has killed," he added, "it's not a big deal to do it again."

I shivered. "Could we talk about Cruz 'n Cuisine?"

If Buzz was surprised or put off, I couldn't tell. "Fortier screwed me," he said flatly. "Just like he did the rest of the kitchen." He snorted indignantly.

The womanizing disgusted Buzz more than Fortier's theft. How was it possible that this man was single, with not even a significant other?

"What happened, exactly?"

"Am I a suspect?" He attempted a return to his light bantering, but he'd lost interest in my hair, perhaps in me. "At this point, aren't we all?" I said flippantly. Whomever the police might suspect, I certainly didn't think I'd suffered some temporary amnesia during which I'd acted out a latent fantasy to kill Fortier. It was equally hard to believe that Buzz Fraser had done it.

Since we couldn't see anything from the balcony, we leaned against the railing and watched the party through the French doors.

"So you want to know the details of my motive?"

"Give me a break, Buzz." I could see how my new endeavor could make enemies and alienate people. Buzz had not quite regained his kidding tone. "I'm new at this." The cold had increased my hunger, and I nervously bit into the sponge cake layered with goo.

"I don't know, Carol. I made the pitch. Everything was going great. Then the station manager dropped me like a hot potato."

"In Eldon's hand," I quipped, a standard kitchen joke. Most of us had scarred, heat resistant hands, whereas Eldon's were renowned for dainty softness.

"Like that," Buzz agreed, seriously. "I thought he'd changed his mind about the program." He shrugged.

I set the cake on the railing and squeezed Buzz. "Do you have any idea why the station manager replaced you?"

He flinched. "My alcohol problem."

I knew about this vaguely. Unlike Fortier, trained by the Culinary Academy, Buzz had learned the trade on the job, starting at the kitchen of a camp, an extension of a dry-out clinic.

"You've been clean a long time, haven't you?"

"I got a D.U.I. last year, Carol."

"I didn't know that." I felt a little queasy.

"Right after the party."

Last year's party had featured a huge, crystal, never-empty punch bowl right where the shrimp were now. Chad and I had come by cab and I'd been somewhere between tipsy and inebriated, but even so I remembered the raucous knot of guys on the balcony. I'd had to restrain Chad from joining them. Red had shouted, "Geronimo," and leaped. Then there'd been the ambulance.

Since Red had only broken his leg and seemed to enjoy being the center of attention, people laughed and joked about the party for weeks. The whole affair had been stupid, but fun. Now, however, I glimpsed a more sinister side to the fizzing, gold liquid and the false insouciance, the temptation they offered to someone like Buzz.

I shook off the guilt. Buzz could have called a cab. I knew why he hadn't, though. He'd fallen off the wagon. He'd screwed up. He'd wanted to escape, unnoticed.

"I had some counseling then, Carol," Buzz said to reassure me. I'd been quiet too long. "I'm not drinking."

His voice sounded unsure, as though the habit were a capricious monkey, tamed and housebroken, but never totally controlled.

I nervously consumed the rest of the petit four. "If I didn't know about your D.U.I., how did Fortier?"

"I'm not sure he knew, Carol. After all, when did Fortier ever need facts?"

"But you think he suggested to the station manager you might not be reliable, that you had an alcohol problem?"

"That's what I think. Then I think Fortier turned on his charm, pulled out his credentials, and said, 'I'm your man,' and it was a done deal."

"You don't sound very bitter." I suddenly felt clammy and nauseous. Saliva pooled in my mouth.

"Oh, I'm bitter, Carol." His body tensed and his voice grew steely. "I've never been any good at expressing stuff, but I feel it with a vengeance." His right hand balled into a fist. "I could have killed Fortier. Easily."

"But you didn't," I blurted, feeling uncomfortable. This was not the Buzz Fraser I knew. "Did you?"

He pointed excitedly through the glass at the package in Eldon's hand. "Come on. That's your present."

Instead, I turned back over the railing and heaved, grateful for the screen of fog.

CHAPTER FOURTEEN

When I finally crawled out of bed the next morning, Chad solicitously brought me a large mug of black French roast.

"Aren't you going to roof today?" I asked Chad. Reinforced by a jolt of caffeine, I stumbled toward the bathroom.

"I thought I'd do something special for you on your day off." He'd been asleep when I'd come home and had no way to know how weak I felt.

I pressed a steaming washcloth to my face. Vomiting was a violent act and even after a night's rest, I felt as wobbly as a colt. Buzz had been great, fetching my gifts, a glass of water, and damp napkins. I contrasted Buzz's care with Chad's state of ignorance, and quite unfairly, found Chad lacking. But I couldn't tell Chad what had happened. He might conclude, as I had, that someone had tried to poison me! Trying to investigate and to deal with Chad's protective reaction would be more than I wanted to take on. Thank God for Buzz's calm response, as though throwing up were as common as sneezing.

"Why?" I asked Chad, but the cloth muffled my question. As a child, I must have driven my mom crazy. Why, why, why. But, maybe not. She had a brain full of proverbs: "Because a stitch in time saves nine," or "Because haste makes waste."

I pulled away the cloth. Chad and Buzz were about the same age, but Chad looked twenty-five rather than thirty-five and had the exuberance of a teenager, although his face at the moment looked crestfallen. Perhaps because I felt weary, I longed for the stolid, older presence of Buzz.

"Why not?" Chad watched me brush my teeth. "Why not take the love of my life on a romantic getaway?"

"That's really thoughtful, Chad." I tried to sound enthusias-
tic, but it was hard to connect "love of my life" with the pallid
face and Bozo-the-Clown hair in the mirror. And a "romantic get
away" could put a damper on my snooping.

I continued brushing my teeth, stalling further discussion.
Chad watched from the doorway as though my rabid, foaming
mouth were sexy.

Alexis had implied that Julieanne Fortier still loved Jean Alcee,
but that only increased the likelihood she'd killed him. No wrath
like that of a woman scorned. Good grief, I sounded like my
mother. I spit and rinsed my mouth. Although Jean had apparently been poisoned in Archibald's kitchen, we did have the mysterious Kris Kringle gift. Eldon insisted Fortier had received a jar
of honey decorated with a holiday ribbon. I simply did not believe Fortier had participated in the gift exchange.

I examined my weary face in the mirror. No zits. The blood-
shot whites of my eyes threw the blue-green irises into high relief.

Detectives Peters and Carman had spent an hour looking for
the elusive jar of honey. Anyone could have given the gift to Jean
Alcee Fortier, including Julieanne. Alexis could have delivered it
for her. Maybe they'd both benefit from his death. If the jar even
existed. Maybe Eldon had invented it to divert attention from
the kitchen's food.

Chad pushed away from the door frame. "I could tell the
C.D. player didn't surprise you."

"I love it." I slipped on my rose-colored, terry robe. "I know
you like it, but it wasn't a surprise."

We walked to the kitchen. "That's okay, Chad. I don't need
to be surprised."

He put the cast iron skillet on a burner, took the cutting
board from the top of the refrigerator, and chopped onion, garlic
and green pepper.

Our tiny maple table had two drop leaves that we kept folded.
The menorah sat in the table's center, my present from Chad's
mom. I hadn't gotten her anything, but Chad had bought her

something and signed the card from both of us. I pulled out a caned chair. In the event of company, we raised the leaves and hauled down two chairs from the attic.

"Who gave you the book?" Chad asked.

"My Kris Kringle." *Armed and Dangerous*, the perfect gift, lay on the free-standing counter. It was a companion book of *Deadly Doses*. My mind drifted back to Buzz, the party, and the murder. I wanted to know for certain whether the honey was a legitimate Kringle gift or not. Especially since it had mysteriously disappeared, and therefore seemed suspicious. Who had participated, who had drawn whom, and was everyone matched?

Chad cracked eggs into a bowl. "Who was your Kris Kringle?"

"Just who you guessed."

He tossed the chopped vegetables into the skillet. They sizzled in hot oil. His back stayed to me.

Chad was predictable. He was chewing on the way I'd discouraged his attendance of the party, but I didn't reassure him. Jealousy was a wild beast, not reined by logic. Any protestations about me and Buzz would only spur the ride.

All week I'd innocently raved about my Kris Kringle gifts. I'd discovered them on my refrigerator shelf, in my locker, and taped to the antenna of my car. "Must be Suzanne," I'd said.

"It's Buzz," Chad had glumly insisted with the intuition of a bared heart.

At the time, I'd shrugged, unsure, or not wanting to deal with it.

The gifts had been intimate, like the large, tortoise shell hair clip. This was someone who knew I wouldn't care for the popular, elasticized ruffles, who knew only a large clip would hold my heavy hair, who sensed I might like to clip my hair although I braided it for work.

Chad added the eggs to the skillet, pressed wheat bread into the toaster, and shredded Monterey Jack cheese.

"So where are we going on our romantic getaway?"

He turned and smiled primly. "It's a surprise."

Chad drove my car rather than his beat-up Ford Ranger, and headed south on coastal Freeway 1. Out my window, wooded hills studded with houses fell away to the ocean. The overcast obscured the outline of Monterey Peninsula curving into the Pacific.

I could have gotten out of the trip if I'd told Chad I'd been sick. I dismissed the idea again. He'd worry too much.

I could count the times I'd thrown up (at least the times I remembered) on one hand. I hadn't eaten anything but one petit four and there wasn't much in sponge cake and sugar that could go bad. A case of food poisoning seemed out of the question.

"Is something wrong?" Chad asked.

"No, nothing, sweetheart." In spite of the cold, morning fog, I rolled down the window. If Chad could intuit something was wrong from my back, I didn't dare look at him.

"I thought you looked pale this morning."

"Tired," I replied, as I concluded all over again that someone had tried to poison me. But why? And if he were going to bother, why not kill me? Whoever our murderer was, he certainly knew how to kill if that's what he wanted.

"That's what I thought," Chad said.

For a moment I imagined Chad was agreeing with my conclusion. I'd lost track of our conversation.

"A relaxing trip is just what you need."

I barely comprehended what he was saying. I recalled Santa Claus, or Eldon as Santa Claus. He'd been specific. *The pink one is for Alexis.*

"Enjoying the view?" Chad asked.

"Oh yes, beautiful."

Why would Eldon want to poison Alexis? There must have been some sort of emetic in the cake. Not lethal, but enough to make a person sick. But why?

"What's wrong?" Chad asked. "You're acting like someone obsessed. Or possessed."

When I turned toward him, I didn't see his face. There, dividing the north and south bound lanes, as Chad exited on to 152, were rows of oleander bushes. Free, available, and very toxic. I couldn't wait to look up oleander in my reference books, not that it was the emetic used on me. Rather, if it produced the flu-like symptoms Jean had experienced, I'd consider making an anonymous phone call to the police. So what if it were far-fetched. Pathologists could detect almost any poison, but it helped if they knew what to look for.

I lay a hand on Chad's thigh to reassure him. "I am obsessed."

Chad exited the freeway onto 152 through downtown Watsonville, which seemed much-recovered from the Loma Prieta earthquake of 1989. Main Street had preserved its turn-of-the-century, western flavor. The new Ford's Department Store bulked, a gray block with too few windows. I had the nagging impression Watsonville had purchased a surplus of orange paint. Before the earthquake, the Mansion House had been painted a salmon orange, and the upscale La Manzana complex a peachy variation. Both had financial problems before the quake. It didn't seem smart to put that curse on the downtown's new anchor store, but there it was—orange, orange trim.

At a diagonal, across the intersection, I saw a familiar figure lounging on a bench of the plaza. "Pull over," I commanded Chad.

I stuck my body far out the window like a rowdy teenager, and waved over the top of the car. "Abundio!" I shouted. He looked around. "Over here, Abundio!"

Chad crossed the intersection, but construction to our right had torn up any possibility of parking on that side of Main Street. "Why do you want to stop?" Chad asked in frustration.

"Talk to Abundio." I looked back. The tall, young dishwasher gazed into the cloudy sky, as though contemplating whether he'd heard the voice of God.

"Doesn't he have an alibi?"

Chad didn't circle the block, and I didn't protest.

"Do you think that's the only reason I'd want to talk to someone?"

We crossed the dried out Pajaro River down into Pajaro. Dilapidated wooden buildings hugged the ground and advertised pan dulce and cerveza.

"Yeah," Chad said grimly. "Lately, that's what I think."

I sighed. Besides irritating my co-workers and endangering myself, my investigation might lead to divorce. But that wouldn't alter my course. I agonized over decisions, but once made, I seldom changed my mind. My mother called this obstinate; I called it persistent.

The small town gave way to the fertile, low lying Pajaro Valley, nurseries and fields. At Prunedale, Chad took Freeway 101 south. Prunedale nestled in the hills to the west. It was a small community and I'd never been there, but it seemed to make local news an inordinate number of times with brush fires, marijuana fields, or substandard camps for migrant workers. In my mind, it was a place for renegades.

After Salinas, 101 flattened into a warm, monotonous stretch to Soledad, where Chad got off and drove like he was looking for something.

"Oh, goodie. A tour of the prison," I joked. "Chad, how did you ever guess?"

He didn't smile. As a matter of fact, his mouth sagged, as though he thought I may have preferred the tour to whatever he had planned. He stopped at Burger King for lunch. Since he'd packed drinks and snacks, it seemed like a suspense-creating diversion. Or, maybe he couldn't go any longer without nicotine. He grabbed a package of Vantage from his shirt pocket before the car door thunked.

After I'd eaten a salad and he'd downed a Whopper and fries, he doubled back on the thoroughfare, turned on a two lane highway and headed into the parched rolling hills, chaparral country, my favorite kind, dotted with scrub oaks.

I'd deduced from an inconspicuous sign that we were on our way to Pinnacles National Monument. Since I'd never been there, my curiosity stirred. The land did not look like it could contain pinnacles. The narrow road through private pastures and over cattle guards didn't lead to any tourist mecca. It was eerily quiet. We didn't pass another car.

The pinnacles appeared suddenly, solid, rocky interruptions of a gentle landscape. Chad pulled into a parking lot, about the size of one for a major supermarket. Besides restrooms, a ranger's station and a few picnic tables, the place remained undeveloped.

"Like it?" Chad asked.

I climbed out, stretched, looked at the few cars in the lot, heard the ugly caw of a jay, distinct and separate in the quiet, and sniffed the sagey air heightened by the smell of coming rain.

"I love it!"

"Better than *Armed and Dangerous?*" he asked wistfully.

CHAPTER FIFTEEN

Four o'clock in the morning was an obscene time to be at work. I climbed the steps to the loading dock, entered the hallway, punched in, and changed into my uniform without waking up. Still somnolent, I dragged myself up the hallway to the entry to the kitchen. I didn't stop at the bakery, but passed through the kitchen, turning left before the pastry department.

I unlocked the first refrigerator, feeling gloomy that we'd had to resort to this after the meat thefts last Christmas. Outside it poured, a great day to be in bed, snuggled with Chad. A half gallon of black olives and a block of feta cheese sat on my shelf. I irritably shoved them aside. They should have been on the chefs' Use-First shelf, but a quick look up told me there wasn't room. I'd bitch later to Eldon. Maybe, if the door weren't always locked, someone would use the stuff, or, at least, clean the shelf.

As I lugged my five gallon bucket of dough and "borrowed" a scoop from the garde manger, I thought of the bed and breakfast in Carmel where Chad had taken me after our hike. We'd dined on our provisions, and the fresh fruit and sherry in the room. And that night, in our haven, we'd listened to the promise and thrum of rain.

I snapped chocolate chip balls on the sheets in rapid-fire motion. Ching, ching, ching. I fantasized about myself with limpid eyes, Chad's strong, warm hand on my soft belly, joy throbbing through his fingers as I announced, "I'm pregnant." I should quit my job, overcome my silly obsession with crime, and have a couple of kids with this dreamy man before time ran out. I resented coming back to this place where someone was mean enough to put an emetic in a petit four. "Where someone is deranged enough to murder," I corrected myself.

On the other hand, I may not have been slamming cookies on the tray because of my return to work, but rather because of the seduction from it. I'd completely lost the momentum of my "investigation." I hadn't even remembered to look up oleander. This brought up the age-old, annoying issue of how one held on to self in relationships. I'd momentarily fallen prey to the idea of depending on someone else's money. And kids? This from a woman who'd seriously considered tubal ligation and religiously downed birth control pills in spite of the risks. Holy moley.

While it'd been enjoyable, no, more than that—supremely delicious—to have Buzz's sweetness inspire Chad to such heights, I could see the situation developing into a real mess.

I took the empty bucket around the corner to Victor and Abundio.

"Buenos dias, amigos."

"Such henerosity," Victor said, rinsing the huge, sticky bucket.

Abundio held up a wet, soapy hand. He was tall and skinny, with lots of freckles, reddish-brown hair, and a big grin. He and Victor didn't look like relatives, but whole strings of people at Archibald's were. Nepotism ran rampant.

"Eh, Carol, know 'y cannibals won't eat clowns?" Victor asked.

I shook my head.

"They tas' funny."

I smiled and ducked back into my niche, still pondering my personal life. I couldn't blame Chad for feeling a bit insecure. With his family, I considered it miraculous that Chad was normal. His mom had abandoned him to her parents on a dairy farm near Ferndale, while she'd drifted around the country, trying to make a living, experimenting with various partners and lifestyles. That's why Chad called his mom Mary. His grandmother was mom.

"Carol."

I jumped and turned.

"Sorry."

Delores stood dejectedly in the entrance. Her large, thick-lashed blue eyes looked red and puffy.

"Whatcha need, Delores?"

She stared at the table, then at the floor. When she raised her head, she looked haunted and ineffably sad, like a deserted child.

How did Fortier do this? How did an average-looking, middle-aged chef command such power over a stunningly beautiful twenty-year-old?

"The melon baller?" she asked.

I glanced guiltily at the still doughy scoop at the end of my table. "Tell Suzanne I'm sorry. I thought I'd be done with it before you missed it. I didn't think we had any melons in December."

A tear leaked down Delores' smooth, olive skin.

"Oh, sweetie . . . ." My heart ached for her. I stopped myself from saying Fortier wasn't worth it, and instead grabbed the folding steps from the hall. "Sit down a bit. Have a good cry."

Her blue eyes widened at the sight of the steps, but she complied. I handed her one of the ubiquitous, small white towels, and noticed a glow-in-the-dark Band-Aid on her plump, childish thumb. But, she didn't cry anymore.

"I better get back before Suzanne gets mad."

"Suzanne will not get mad."

Of everyone in the kitchen, Suzanne had the evenest temper. She was the only one of us that I'd describe as sweet. Even Delores had flared up when she thought Fortier's eyes were roving, as no doubt they had been. How did a possessive twenty-year-old deal with the fact her boyfriend had once been her mom's lover, I wondered.

"Are you okay?" Delores now asked me.

"I just had a surprising thought." I didn't tell Delores it was about her. What if she'd only recently learned about her mom and Fortier? She would have been a child back then, and Esperanza struck me as a private, discreet person. Could such a discovery provoke a fiery, jealous girl to kill? I reminded myself of my basic contention: anyone could kill if the circumstances were right.

I did a quick look-see into the kitchen. Eldon hovered by the frantic Ray on the front line. The front line demanded a great deal more skill and timing than the mass cooking in the back line, and Ray had not been properly trained. Like several others, he'd been tossed into his new position by Fortier's death and was learning the job under pressure.

In spite of Eldon's preoccupation, he could bounce over to the bakery at any moment. I had to give him credit; he kept the employees on their toes.

"Let's give Suzanne the melon baller and punch out for an official break."

Delores agreed. "No offense, Carol, but this room gives me the creeps."

Now that Big Red had taken Ray's place on the back line, Suzanne's cousin worked in the Employees' Dining Room or in kitchen lingo, the EDR. We were used to the musical chairs, as the kitchen operated on the burn and turn principle: Burn 'em out and turn 'em over. Suzanne's cousin was a blonder, bustier, brassier version of Suzanne and had caused many minor cases of whiplash in the kitchen.

Delores and I filled paper cups full of coffee and Delores picked up a couple of my overdone spice cookies that'd been relegated to E.D.R. We sat in the corner furthest from the steam table.

"Would you happen to know the last thing Fortier ate before he died?"

A blush grew from the top of her chef's smock to the bottom of her white hat. The question had been blunt, but I didn't see anything embarrassing about it.

"I meant food," I stammered, suddenly feeling like an idiot. "Do you know what food he ate last? Excluding the lebkuchen dough he may have sampled."

She nodded, and the blush deepened a shade.

Now I was confused. "Well, what?"

She squinched her face and squirmed in her seat.

"Tell me," I coaxed.

She shook her head.

"Come on. I won't tell anyone."

"Honey," she croaked.

I nodded, eager and waiting. The information fit perfectly with my brilliant deductions.

She scooted the cafeteria chair closer and whispered, "We went in the walk-in cooler."

This particular Fortier ploy had become part of the initiation rite for every female employee. Many years ago, for me, it had been instructive. When Fortier had led me from the cooler, I'd felt the half dozen sets of eyes on my nipples, and since then I'd managed, in spite of Fortier's good looks, abundant energy, and impressive knowledge of cooking, never to forget how juvenile he could be. My vigilance never prevented incidents like the one in the locker room, but I'd circumvented a lot by not being alone with the guy and not passing him in the tighter spots of the kitchen. I felt guilty for not warning Delores, when on her first day, she had emerged in the puff of cold fog, nodding solemnly and asking about the labels.

"At first it was like a picnic," Delores continued. She had no discernible accent, but her voice had a muted quality, a lack of explosive b's and p's, probably learned from her mother. "He was eating the honey on your scones, 'cept he said they were bitter like you didn't stir in the soda good." Delores lowered her eyes.

I thought badly of the dead. Fortier had snitched those scones from the bakery. My scones were too popular to end up in the EDR. The nerve of him saying they were bitter!

"Then . . . ." She blushed furiously. "He wanted to put the honey . . . on my . . . ." She giggled, the nervous sound of a modest person. "I couldn't."

Part of her embarrassment stemmed from her inability to accommodate Fortier. Hatred of the guy erupted in me like torched kerosene. He'd taken an innocent, possibly virginal young lady, and made her feel ashamed of her purity.

"But he did eat more honey?" I pressed.

She winced. "From my nipples."

CHAPTER SIXTEEN

I glanced at the clock up on the wall behind the steam table. "We'd better get back." We were entitled to two fifteen-minute breaks. I was enough of a one-person show to take them back to back, but Delores was new and vulnerable. She couldn't afford for Eldon to write her up.

We tucked our politically correct paper, as opposed to styrofoam, cups into the garbage can. "Did Fortier get sick right after that?"

"I'm not sure. We can't see the line chefs from the garde manger, and we're not on the route to the bathroom."

I made a mental note to ask Eldon about how and when Fortier had gotten sick.

We exited the cafeteria atmosphere into a tacky hallway. Across from the EDR were the locker room, the employee restrooms, and then the swinging door into the kitchen. The hall dead-ended in a storage room.

"Where'd he get the honey?" I asked.

"I think from Tio Victor," she said.

I stopped with my hand on the door into the kitchen and shushed her. This was a new twist. We were about to enter near the dishwashers, but Delores hadn't shown the slightest hesitancy in mentioning Victor.

"Why you want me to be quiet?" she whispered.

She evidently had not grasped the possible connection between the honey and Fortier's death. However, the murderer certainly knew the connection and might not appreciate others paying to much attention to it.

I backed away from the door, so it wouldn't swing out and hit me in the face.

"Tio Victor keeps bees," she explained in a low voice, baffled by my behavior.

I pushed her back toward the supply room. "Promise me you'll keep our conversation a secret."

"Gawd," she said, wrinkling her nose. "You think I'm gonna tell people 'bout that?"

"Don't tell anybody about any of it."

I wondered if my advice could be considered an obstruction to justice. Certainly Delores should tell the police, but I could not imagine Victor giving Fortier anything but a sock in the jaw. If he had given the honey to Fortier, it would have been to kill him.

"You're not sure the honey was from Victor?"

"It was a Kris Kringle present." She frowned, uncertain why I belabored this point, and nervously picked at the Band-Aid on her thumb. "We sorta got in a fight about it because Jean wouldn't let me see the tag."

"Tag?" I asked excitedly.

"On the ribbon. Jean told me it was from his secret admirer. He did that to make me mad, I know."

I realized why she hadn't connected the honey and the death. She wasn't dumb. She was too innocent to imagine murder. She might be in for a shock when the police reported the autopsy results. Fortier's death had been, to her, an inexplicable act of God.

"Delores, what happened to the jar of honey?"

"I don't know. I left first."

Something was happening to me. My heart banged. Adrenaline and endorphins shot like starbursts through my body. The excitement was like a drug rush. What if Fortier knew he'd been poisoned, had sat on my stool because he could go no farther, and put his finger in my dough, not to sample it, but rather, knowing it was full of molasses and honey, to point at it, a desperate, last minute message?

Delores's big blue eyes anxiously switched across my face a couple of times and then looked over the wire shelves, the stacks of plates and trays.

The idea of Fortier Kris Kringling didn't ring true, but I knew what I had to do to confirm my suspicion. "Just out of curiosity, Delores, whose name did you draw?"

"I had Patsy," she said puzzled. "Actually I drew Suzanne's name, but Eldon wanted to switch."

That made sense. Eldon would be at a loss for what to get Patsy. On the other hand, his eyes tracked Suzanne whenever she trotted across the kitchen.

I pushed open the door. "Who had your name, Delores?"

"Ray."

All through my shift, I stayed wired as though on a double expresso. After that, I returned to the EDR for lunch, my eyes darting with suspicion, seeing the room and people as though for the first time. A line filed before the shiny stainless steel table with its Plexiglas sneeze guards. The aromas of leftover prime rib and horseradish crowded the small, warm room. I knew most of the people only vaguely, since they were from the on-coming shift. I started and finished earlier than my co-workers. However, Buzz stood in line, in uniform, taking a late break. He turned and winked at me. My heart did a weird little soft shoe with cane and top hat.

Since the party, something had changed in our relationship and I didn't like it. I wanted the good old days when a wink was just a wink.

I took a plastic plate from the shelf, but waved people ahead of me, as I stalled, hoping Alexis would show. Being focused, or, according to my mom stubborn and obsessive, I needed to let go of my initial suspicion of Julieanne (and, maybe, by extension, Alexis), before I could focus on this new twist—the honey from the supposed Kris Kringle. Uncle Victor?

I had shed my uniform and slipped on dusty rose sweats, but the tight braid of my hair pulled on my scalp and I looked forward to the tingling pleasure of its release. My mouth salivated at the smell of the succulent meat, until I remembered the last time I'd eaten at work, the petit four at the party. Nausea fluttered through my belly.

The guy at the end of the line turned to me. "Dead meat," he said disgustedly.

I wondered if I were to infer that he preferred it still pulsating.

"I guess you don't feel like eating either," he said, as the line moved and I hung back.

He was tall, thin and anemic-looking. I thought some red meat might do him good. "We have incisors for ripping meat from bone," I mumbled.

"Oh, one of those," the cadaver said disdainfully. He stepped forward and inspected the cases for dead plants to eat.

I made a face at his back. What an asshole. He didn't even care that I thought most Americans gorged themselves on red meat, clogged their arteries and seriously affected the ability of the planet to provide for others, and that I ate meat only at special times like this.

I was standing on tiptoes to see how much prime rib remained when Alexis hustled into the room, in uniform but out of breath. I stepped into the line. Alexis, preoccupied with the clock, grabbed a plate and stood behind me.

I turned. "Hi, Alexis."

"Oh, hi, Carol." She jiggled the plate in one hand and the fingers of the other rubbed the thumbnail.

I inched forward and spooned rosemary potatoes on to my plate. In sotto voce, I said, "I was very interested in our discussion the other night."

Alexis's dark eyes darted around the room and she spotted Buzz at a table. She nearly dropped the cheap plate allotted employees for exactly that reason.

I tonged broccoli flowers and Alexis followed suit. "I was hoping I could meet Julieanne. Talk to her."

"She left," Alexis said.

"Left?" I echoed. Her action screamed guilty like a neon pink bulletin. It seemed abrupt, a definite reaction. On the other hand, my progress had been sluggish. Ten days had passed since Fortier had been murdered in the bakery. I also had the nagging detail of the honey. If it had been the vehicle, how had Julieanne gotten the poisoned product into the kitchen? How had she known to disguise it as a Kringle present?

"She went back to New Orleans," Alexis said bitterly. I wondered what the cops would make of that.

Alexis forked a slab of meat on to her plate and was finished. Her eyes flicked over the nearly full room, to where Buzz sat alone. I wondered if she'd get up the courage to sit with him, and where I could go if she did. As Alexis stood mired in personal crisis, her guard down, I asked, "Do you know who'll inherit Jean's condo?"

"Me." She looked up at me, her eyes fearful, but whether about the condo or sitting with Buzz, I didn't know. I led the way to his table, deciding to eat fast.

"Did your uncle leave a will?"

"What?" Her fingers tightened on her tray, and her eyes dropped to the floor.

I pitied her. No member of the opposite sex had ever reduced me to a bumbling stupor, although I'd once had a confusing crush on a guy, who, I later realized was my brother Donald's first boyfriend.

"A will?" I prodded, as we seated ourselves at Buzz's table. Buzz and I exchanged glances. Alexis said nothing. I felt like kicking her. I did. Fast and friendly under the table.

"No, uhm," she said, as though prodded from a slumber. "He had one of those things, a living trust." Resentful eyes locked on mine.

So she knew Fortier was leaving her yacht harbor property. No wonder she'd called him generous.

I stood with my plate. The chocolate brown eyes panicked.

"No offense," I said, "but I've decided to eat outside."

Buzz looked at me like I was crazy, a completely logical response I realized when I stepped into a misty rain. I gulped lunch and went home to make a phone call.

CHAPTER SEVENTEEN

As it turned out, what the police made of Julieanne's disappearance was nothing much.

"We have no reason to suspect her," the nice Detective Carman told me over the phone. Without the autopsy results, I supposed they couldn't officially suspect anyone. In the meantime, ten days had passed. Today was the 29th. The killer had had a lot of time to cover his or her tracks.

Detective Carman thanked me. I grabbed my book *Deadly Doses* and wandered to the backyard, feeling like an idiot. Had I expected them to send a posse galloping to New Orleans?

If only gangs could practice restraint, I thought. Poison would be so much more efficient than drive-by shootings. With a little arsenic in the pozole, the Watsonville rival gangs of Northside and Poorside could wipe out one another, and the whole affair might be passed off as a bad batch of chorizo.

In our tiny backyard, as in the front, Chad and I had foregone any attempt at a lawn and had opted for an English garden, a flagstone path through wildflowers and drought-resistant perennials. Along the redwood fence hung baskets of fuchsias, chenille plants, and pelargoniums.

I lounged on the brick landing. Lola curled around my butt, but acted as if I weren't there, as though she had to sneak up on me or I'd move, a reasonable deduction since I often hopped up to do things in a manner that mystified even my husband.

Chad had hoisted Lola from a free box at the flea market because he felt sorry for her. Back then, I'd made some snide comment about picking the ugliest one he could find.

Now I scratched under her neon pink flea collar and slathered affection. "Oh, Lola, you're so cute."

She purred and squeezed her round green eyes shut in ecstasy, then stretched, arching, as if to say, "Of course."

I leafed through *Deadly Doses*, as I had a perverse aversion to tables of contents. I found oleander under Poisonous Plants, Quickly Fatal, after monkshood and before paternoster pea. In Sanskrit the plant's name meant "Horse Killer," in Arabic and Italian "Ass Killer." Well, that was appropriate.

Could the killer have selected the poison for its meaning? The twisted wit appealed to me, but I couldn't imagine anyone, except maybe myself, doing something like that in real life.

On a scale of one to six, nerium oleander had a toxicity of six with a reaction time of twenty to forty minutes. A native of Asia, it had been introduced as an ornamental shrub in the United States. All parts were deadly, including the nectar of the flower, smoke from a burning plant, or water in which the flowers had been placed.

The drug stimulated the heart, causing sweating, vomiting, bloody diarrhea, unconsciousness, respiratory paralysis and death.

In Europe, oleander was used as rat poison.

The next line popped my eyes. When bees used oleander pollen for their honey, the honey could be poisonous.

Maybe there was no mystery at all. Victor, the patriarch of the Medina family, felt protective of Delores. He made certain his bees sucked up oleander nectar. Then, he slipped Fortier, the womanizer, the ass, a jar of his special product.

CHAPTER EIGHTEEN

I didn't want to talk to Eldon. It pissed me off that he'd handed me those petit fours with such ingenuousness, even though I didn't think he'd doctored them. The reason I dreaded the conversation was that Eldon had no life except Archibald's. He tended to be officious, and long-winded, his good intentions spilled out in the latest managerial jargon.

As far as I knew, Eldon didn't take breaks, and he ate his lunch in the mid-afternoon during the lull in customers. However, he arrived about six and he did eat breakfast.

So, the next morning I caught Eldon in the EDR hunched over three pieces of French toast swimming in maple syrup. He had one of my leftover apricot Danishes on the side and a cup of coffee that looked as though it were half cream. I bet it had three or four sugars in it, too.

I got a cup of coffee and straddled a chair at his table, my elbows on its back. I wanted the little physical barrier between us, so that hopefully I could extract myself more easily. "One quick question, Eldon."

He made a motion for me to turn the chair and patted the table, but I acted ignorant of sign language. He chewed meticulously, swallowed, and dabbed his mouth. "You have fifteen minutes, Carol. Relax." He saw no irony in his statement. With his fork and knife he cut a perfect, fat wedge of French toast. "I've been thinking of organizing a stress management workshop for the employees. I've noticed that some of the staff have been very stressed by what happened."

What happened, I thought. Talk about glossing over—no

mention of Fortier or death, not even a euphemism like passed away.

"Delores, in particular, although she's not the only one. Esperanza seems distraught, too. Have you noticed?"

Distraught was too histrionic for the stoic Esperanza. "She's probably worried about Delores," I said.

"Buzz, too," he hummed, thoughtfully twirling a forkful of cooked bread in the syrup.

Two words. Buzz, too. That was completely unlike Eldon. I looked at him, but he simply watched back. We both tried to read the other. "Buzz seems distraught?"

"I guess you haven't noticed . . . ." His voice drifted, but just as I opened my mouth to pop my question, he boldly asserted, "You seem a little hyper yourself, Carol."

"I'm okay," I said bluntly.

"I know this group from San Jose. They're very good."

I watched hopefully as he more firmly speared the goo-soaked wedge in preparation to lift it.

"I attended one of their seminars called 'Stress for Success.'"

"Interesting concept," I muttered.

That was the wrong thing to say. It encouraged him, but I could hardly tell my boss to shut up and listen while I asked him one simple question.

"It focused on how to convert stress to drive, rather than how to get rid of stress." Now he drove the wedge of French toast through the brown puddle as though it were a toy boat. "I think I could get Archibald's to spring for the cost." The bread went round and round in the brown puddle. He didn't plan to pop it into his mouth until he finished talking, which could be the next blue moon. "We could probably . . . ."

"Eldon," I interjected assertively, "excuse me. I'm sorry to interrupt, but I have to get back to work."

He glanced at his digital watch. "You still have seven minutes, Carol." He chose this moment to stick the French toast into his mouth.

"When and how did Fortier get sick?"

His light brown eyes looked at me inquisitively as the smooth, pale face moved to his patient, thorough chewing.

"I'm surprised the incident has agitated you so much, Carol. I mean, certainly, it was a shock for everyone, but I didn't think you and Fortier were friendly, actually the opposite. I frankly don't believe the police's insinuations, but if I had to choose someone, to well, ehm, ..." He cleared his throat.

I restrained from clutching my forehead and moaning. Usually I escaped these "conversations" by leaving, but now I needed information. "When did Fortier get sick?" I persisted.

"Right after his break," Eldon said. "He and Delores were in the cooler, fooling around." He smacked his lips, furrowed his brow, and shook his head at their juvenile behavior.

I was stunned to hear Eldon make such a personal remark. "Didn't you mind?"

He shrugged. "They both punched out. If a guy's going through a mid-life crisis and needs to act like a teenager, as long as he does it on his time, that's his problem."

"And how did he get sick?"

"Well, in spite of the police's insinuations, I never thought for a moment, Carol, that it was caused by *our kitchen* or your lebkuchen. I hope . . . ."

"Eldon," I interrupted bravely.

His smooth forehead puckered, and, almost as a reflex, he checked his watch.

"Eldon," I interrupted again, feeling trapped, frantic and irritated. "I meant how was Fortier sick. Did he vomit or what?"

Eldon wrinkled his nose. "He was sweating and his breathing was ragged. He said he felt very ill and needed to go home. I offered to call a taxi; I really didn't think he should try to drive, but then he rushed off; I assumed to the restroom and I assumed to vomit. I didn't see him after that. Until, of course, Patsy found him."

He checked his watch.

"Thanks," I said abruptly. "Oh, yeah, Eldon, would you tell the cooks to keep their use-first stuff off my shelf?" Before he could reply, I bailed.

CHAPTER NINETEEN

"Ah shit," I thought, as I went out the EDR door. I'd forgotten to ask Eldon about his Kris Kringle. I knew he'd exchanged with Delores to get Suzanne's name, but who'd drawn his name?

If I could determine for certain who'd given Fortier the present, I'd be a step closer to solving the mystery. Delores thought the honey was her Uncle Victor's, but she may have jumped to that conclusion simply because he kept bees. Or did the jar have distinguishing characteristics? Even so, the murderer could have used Victor's honey to point suspicion at Victor.

Eldon's description of Fortier's symptoms fit my reference books' descriptions of oleander poisoning. My guess was that the killer had put oleander in the honey, possibly via bees, and Fortier had been murdered with sweetness. He'd licked the ambrosia from the horns of plenty and was very sick by the time he walked to the kitchen.

As I moved down the cold hallway, I shivered. Killing someone with a Christmas gift seemed cold-blooded, even to me. The aroma of my garlic/rosemary bread wafted down the tiled corridor. Under the pungent bouquet, the yeasty warmth comforted me like a prenatal memory of my mother's fragrance.

I contemplated the phone in the hall. I wanted to make my anonymous tip now, before I lost my nerve. I went into the restroom, yanked a wad of toilet paper, and returned to the phone. I pulled up the unwieldy directory by its chain, balanced it on a raised knee, and looked up the Santa Cruz Police Department's tip line. The book said "anonymous crime information," but I wasn't taking any chances. Feeling like a gangster, I covered the mouthpiece with the toilet paper. I nervously scanned the hallway as I listened to the recorded message in English and then in Spanish. Then I blurted that they should have the pathologist working on the Fortier case check for oleander poisoning.

I slammed down the receiver and wiped my sweaty palm on my houndstooth pants. I didn't like talking on the phone in the best of circumstances, which this wasn't.

When I pushed through the door into the kitchen, Abundio and Victor had arrived and were busy cleaning bowls and plates and doughy vats from the bakery. A short conveyor belt ran a rubber rack into a dishwasher, more for sterilizing than cleaning. Abundio and Victor rinsed everything first, and they grappled with the big pots and bowls by hand. They turned from their clatter and steam to greet me.

I didn't even say hola. I said, "Did you guys participate in the Kris Kringle?"

They both looked startled. To make sure he'd correctly interpreted the English, Abundio looked to Victor who repeated the question to him in Spanish. They looked quizzically at each other, and then back at me.

"Yes," Victor said. "I had Ray's name."

That didn't, I thought, preclude him from giving Fortier a jar of honey. Victor was five foot eight so his narrowed, dark eyes skewered mine. A sinister image of Victor formed: he lounged on a Watsonville stoop, wearing a t-shirt and baggies with a butterfly knife in the pocket, a blue bandanna around his forehead, and guns in the trunk of his lowered burgundy Impala.

I shook away the silly stereotype. This was Victor, a man with whom I'd worked for two years, and swapped jokes.

"Who drew your name?"

He jerked a meaty thumb at Abundio. "The Kid."

Abundio grinned. A square Band-Aid covered his freckled wrist.

"What happened there?" I asked.

"Steam burn."

"Just a sec, guys." I turned the corner to check the bread. It needed about five minutes. I didn't wear a watch, for the same reason I didn't wear my wedding ring, and Eldon insisted there be no clock in the kitchen. He didn't want employees watching it. I broke off a piece of my aloe vera plant for Abundio. My accurate internal clock told me I should be mixing the dough for raspberry brochee.

Still, I returned to the dishwashers. "Just one more thing." God, I sounded like Columbo. Well, I adored the rumpled sleuth, so no wonder. I handed Abundio the oozing piece of succulent which he accepted matter-of-factly. Everyone in the kitchen humored my belief in aloe vera juice; some even swore by it. "Who drew your name, Abundio?"

His green eyes lit up. "Suzanne."

Victor reached up and throttled the thin neck. "The Kid he has all the luck."

I felt a nanosecond of annoyance at the unanimous adoration of Suzanne. Surely the woman had a flaw. Perhaps she was a murderess.

I took the dozen steps back to the bakery, my head swimming with information. I needed to write it down. I flipped through my notebook, looking for an unfashionable recipe to use as scratch paper. Maybe something fried. People would rather clog their arteries with cheesecake.

Eldon caught me in the act. "The bread smells great, Carol." He sniffed elaborately. "But I don't smell any brochee."

"I was contemplating something different."

He rounded the work table and looked over my shoulder. "Peanut butter finger crunches," he exclaimed. "Those are too much work, Carol. People love your brochee." He glanced at his watch. "But you need to get on those if we're going to have them for the breakfast bunch."

He was bouncing away when I forced myself to say, "Eldon, who drew your name for the Kris Kringle?"

The big man turned as gracefully as a ballerina. "Todd," he said assiduously. His mouth puckered as though he'd sucked a lemon. "Carol, I don't know what you're up to, but your job here is to bake, not to investigate."

"Yes, boss," I said without even a wee bit of sarcasm. Eldon stood in the entrance for several seconds, looking sternly at me. "I saw you making that call in the hall."

My heart slid to the neighborhood of my big toes, and heat squirted through my body. "I was on break."

"You were five minutes over."

I didn't know how he'd seen me, but fortunately he seemed not to have heard the call. At worst, he'd write me up. I wanted to say, "Hey, Eldon, write me up and leave me alone," but that would have left him no choice but to do it. Most of the time, like now, he only flexed his muscles. He pursed his lips and didn't say anything. The silence was truly disconcerting.

When he finally left, I pulled the recipe from its plastic sheath, but decided it would be safer if I waited until my next break to make the chart.

Later, in the EDR, on my second break, I used the blank side of the recipe to list the morning kitchen employees at the time of the murder and who they'd drawn:

Me - Esperanza
Delores - Patsy
Patsy - ?
Eldon - Suzanne
Buzz - Me
Suzanne - Abundio
Esperanza - ?
Abundio - Victor
Victor - Ray
Ray - Delores
Todd - Eldon
Fortier - ?
Big Red (then in EDR) - ?

When I looked over the chart, I felt sick. I couldn't believe any of these people had murdered Fortier, but worse than that, everyone in the kitchen had been put at risk. Anyone could have tasted the honey and died. Well, maybe not. While Fortier had cruised the kitchen, sampling everything, he'd never shared. His tightness, not his digit in my dough, had pissed me off. Yet, his niece claimed he was generous, and the insurance policy showed a financial generosity toward his wife, and he was generous with the time and attention he gave Concepción. Maybe he was a skinflint only in the realm of his career.

I sipped some water and crunched my pencil, savoring the slightly bitter flavor of wood and graphite. After working around sweets all morning, I didn't relish the snacks in the Employees Dining Room. I had the place to myself, except for the new, knock-out EDR cook, who was busy setting up the steam table for lunch. The noisy rattle of the steam table trays comforted me, but the squeak of her soles on the black and white tiles annoyed me, the way a paper cut would, the way this whole damn business did.

CHAPTER TWENTY

I had to give the police credit. They reacted promptly to my tip. The next day, the last day of the year, the homicide detectives returned to the kitchen. The woman wore a London Fog raincoat and the Detective Carman wore a black windbreaker. Both were sprinkled with rain. Eldon fluttered nervously around them.

The large female, Detective Peters, stood by her partner with legs apart, her arms crossed over her chest, and her weight rocked back in her solid shoes. The kitchen employees circled the two like piranhas.

"This is a holiday," Eldon protested. "We're booked by Apple Computers." He stalked the perimeter of the gathering. "We have seven hundred for dinner."

He seemed more agitated than usual.

"Poison," Detective Peters said.

"Poison," Eldon echoed.

I smiled smugly, but I noticed they weren't saying what type of poison. I felt a chill. They probably considered the type of poison one of those niggly details only the murderer would know. I gulped as though trying to swallow a hard-boiled egg. What if the poison had been oleander?

What if they figured out that I'd made the call?

Eldon waved a pudgy hand to dismiss the ludicrous idea of poison. "Not in this kitchen."

I was amazed at his innocence. Then I realized it was an act. We did, indeed, have poison in the kitchen—rodent killer, that we put on the loading dock.

The female partner, Detective Peters, gave me a long, curious look, a full ten seconds of undivided perusal. I stared back, as is

my style. She had freckled skin, hazel eyes—more green than
brown—and short hair that could be called blonde or light brown.
I felt my friends and colleagues looking at me, too, as the idea of
murder began to take hold. They took their cues from this woman,
considered my knowledge of poisons, and suspected me. The
uneasiness welled around me like a fence. Unfortunately, I could
stare down only one person at a time.

As Eldon swished his hand to wave us back to work, Detective Peters raised hers. I knew the gesture meant STOP from childhood books, but it apparently also communicated well with the
under-thirty group and with the Mexicans.

In spite of the authoritative signal, Eldon frantically mouthed
to Buzz, "The soufflés," and Buzz discretely peeled from the group,
followed by Ray. Buzz had replaced Fortier and Ray had been
promoted from the back line to take Buzz's place.

Detective Peters noticed, but didn't object. After all, they were
in sight and could easily hear from their stations. And probably
she appreciated a light soufflé as much as anyone. Detective Carman
also moved through the circle of bodies, apparently to poke around
the kitchen for a cache of poison leaves.

"To get back to your point, Mr. Dunn, we don't think Mr.
Fortier intentionally or accidentally ate poison in the kitchen.
We're investigating his death as a homicide."

Delores gasped. The eyes that hadn't already pinned me as a
prime suspect hopped around the circle, as if to spot the mania-
cal glaze of the killer's. Eldon stopped fidgeting and quieted, as
though already composing the vaguest possible press release.

"Mr. Fortier had purged his stomach, so the autopsy didn't
reveal much besides the poison," Detective Peters said.

"Purged his stomach?" I asked. "Was Fortier a bulimic?" Terms
like "threw up" might not be pretty, but they sure were a lot
clearer than "purged."

"He vomited," Detective Peters retorted. "In spite of this, the
coroner did find traces of honey."

Detective Peters turned her suspicious, and now pissed-off,

eyes my way. Again the small mob took its cues from her and a dozen pairs of vigilante eyes targeted me.

This was ridiculous. "Look," I said, "if I'd put poison in my lebkuchen, I would have knocked off half our clientele, not just *Mr.* Fortier."

I had a good idea where and how he'd ingested the poison, but I thought Delores ought to tell them about that.

Detective Peters made another abrupt stop sign and I expected her to say, "Achtung!" Instead she droned, "We're not making accusations, Ms. . . . ." She thought a moment about her notes, ". . . Sabala."

Her fair face went through the mental gyrations I'd seen hundreds of times during my life. She didn't ask the usual, "What nationality is that?" so possibly she'd skipped to the next step of altering her stereotypes to include a tall, auburn-haired, Americanized, blue-green eyed Hispanic, or Detective Peters had taken the path of less resistance and decided (erroneously) that Sabala was my married name. Regardless, I felt flattered that she'd memorized my name, yet hoped that didn't mean she was giving me extra attention.

"That's what he got from his Kris Kringle," Delores said softly. All eyes turned to her.

"That's right," Detective Peters commented neutrally.

"A little jar with red and white ribbon around it. It looked homemade like Tio Victor's." She stopped for a moment as the righteous eyes of the crowd rolled toward her uncle.

Victor shrank.

"I mean, at first, I thought Tio Victor must be his Kris Kringle, but now that I know Jean . . . ." She bit her full lips. " . . . was murdered with the honey, I know it couldn't have been Tio Victor."

"Victor had my name," Ray piped in.

The severe greenish eyes of Detective Peters turned to him. "Did he give you any honey?"

Ray gulped. "Well . . .yeah. But it had a blue ribbon on it."

"That's true," Delores said hopefully. "Tio Victor wouldn't put a red ribbon on nothing."

My stereotype of Victor may not have been so far off the mark. From living in California and being more interested in crime than most, I knew the Norteños claimed red and the number fourteen, supposedly for N, the fourteenth letter of the alphabet. The Sureños claimed blue and thirteen for the M of Mexico.

"Where is the honey, Mr. . . . ?"

"Fitzgerald," Ray volunteered. "In my locker."

Officer Carman appeared beside Ray and escorted him toward the locker room.

Everyone waited for more. "And you, . . . Ms. Medina," Detective Peters said impatiently, "what happened with this red-ribboned honey?"

"Jean ate it with scones. He wanted me to try it."

Esperanza blanched and closed her eyes. "Aiieee."

"Of course I didn't."

"Why not?" Detective Peters asked suspiciously.

"I'm allergic to honey."

Detective Peters furiously scribbled notes while the rest of us digested this detail. Eldon was moving nervously from foot to foot and had grown a mustache of perspiration. "Vista Dining Room is sold out tonight," he muttered to the female cop.

I looked over my shoulder. Triumphantly carrying a jar of honey in an evidence bag, her partner returned through the swinging door by the sinks. Ray followed with a sheepish look and mumbled to all of us, "That's been in my locker the whole time."

"Detective," Eldon said, like a boy who desperately needed permission for the restroom.

Peters turned back to him. She was nearly as tall as he, but looked solid, while Eldon looked like an inflated dough boy. "We appreciate the fact you have a busy kitchen to run. We hope to interrupt its operation as little as possible, but we do have a homicide investigation here. Let me make it clear, too, that we have no way of knowing if the poison was administered with the honey."

Her skepticism didn't ring true.

But I knew the poison had not been administered with the honey in the baggy. Someone had known the poisoned honey might point toward Victor, and had made the effort to change the ribbon on the jar.

"We invite all of you to come to the station voluntarily for questioning. We would, at some point, like to talk to all of you, if you know something, or even *think* you *might* know something."

She smiled sardonically and the mossy eyes looked right at me. "Or, if you're guilty."

CHAPTER TWENTY-ONE

I got lucky. There were twenty-five Medinas in the phone book, but only one Victor and he had his address listed. I put on my black sweat pants and red hooded sweatshirt. I thought twice about wearing red, but decided I was being paranoid. The hood would hide my distinctive hair and protect me from rain although the day was now bright after the morning's sprinkle.

I was going to drive out to Watsonville to see if Victor Medina kept bees at his home, and, maybe, with luck, to see where they fed. During the drive, I sorted through my logic, trying not to be distracted by the fluffy clouds and the crisp colors of the ocean. Everything smelled like fresh soil.

The one person with whom Fortier had tried to share his honey, didn't, and wouldn't, sample it. A coincidence? As far as I knew, my heroines didn't believe in them.

If I assumed Delores's allergy to honey was not a coincidence, where did that leave me? Did Delores kill Fortier, using a food she'd not be expected to taste? That didn't seem likely. It didn't make sense, even if she'd found out about her mom and Fortier. Why would she use a food that called attention to herself? Besides, her sorrow convinced me. On the other hand, what did I know of her acting ability? As someone who'd never been dissembling, I didn't readily recognize it. The first time I'd been told that gullible had been removed from the dictionary, I hadn't known it was a joke. I hadn't even known my brother was gay until he'd decided to tell me.

Other people might have thought specifically to protect Delores from Fortier, like say, for example, her mom. Eldon had called Esperanza distraught. For all his conversational ineptitude,

Eldon made accurate assessments of employees and situations. Maybe Esperanza was distraught. Maybe she had more on her mind than Delores's depression. But, then we had Tio Victor, who would not only want to protect Delores, but also farmed bees.

I found Marchant Street and followed the numbers down. Some of the houses were shabby and peeling, others painstakingly cared for. This was a hopeful neighborhood of upward bound immigrants, homeowners with a nice car here and there, a satellite dish occupying one front lawn, pink flamingos in the rose beds of another. Graffiti blighted fences and sides of buildings in the alleys, but the neighborhood lacked the desperate poverty found across the bridge or in the migrant camps. Now, in the mid-afternoon, the area was quiet and peaceful. By nightfall, though, some drunken fool would be shooting a gun into the air. Since bullets, like everything else, responded to gravity, Russian Roulette would have been a simpler and fairer way to celebrate New Year's Eve.

Victor's house was the last on the street before it dead-ended at the levee. It was a white house with two neat squares of shriveled lawn. No car sat in the stubby driveway before the detached garage, and nobody peeked from the windows as I parked my Karmann Ghia.

I slammed the car door, but still no one stirred. I kept on my sunglasses and flipped up the hood of my sweatshirt. I rang the doorbell and waited. Nobody answered, but I felt as though I were being watched. My eyes flicked to the big window to my left, but the beige curtain didn't stir. I was paranoid.

I scrambled up the embankment. My heart pounded with nervousness and excitement. What I was about to do probably constituted stupidity, but I was enjoying the pumped-up, adrenaline rush. I felt sixteen again. I wondered if Fortier experienced the same thrill on his forays into the refrigerator. I also wondered if I were having some sort of early, mid-life crisis.

On top of the levee a concrete bike and walking path followed the curve of the river as far as I could see. A trickle of water flowed through thick brush. I viewed the expanse of Victor's back yard.

A little goat ran around in the center, bleating and bunting at a dodging terrier. The "yard" looked like a half acre, with a chicken coop and barn at the far end. A pebbled, concrete patio guarded the weathered back door, flanked on both sides by a riot of plants, both potted and in the ground. The six-foot, redwood fence kept the goat and dog and chickens from racing off along the river, but certainly was no deterrent to an able-bodied person, offering ample knotholes for toe holds and a flat, two-by-four top on to which I hoisted myself. I thanked kitchen work for my upper body strength and volleyball for my awesome legs. The little dog looked harmless, but I kissed to him to made sure. He bounded toward me, pink tongue lolling and stubby tail wagging.

I dropped into the yard, and a bomb exploded on the back of my head.

CHAPTER TWENTY-TWO

Bugs skittered over my neck and face, but I couldn't move. Something wet, rough and smelly lapped at my cheek.

"Quién es?" a woman asked.

"Some white chick." The voice sounded young and mystified, but it confirmed what I'd always suspected. Mexicans didn't see anything Mexican in me, either.

The woman demanded, like mothers everywhere, for an explanation. In Spanish she asked why he'd hit me.

"I didn't hit her," the boy retorted defensively in English.

"Dìmelo en español!" The mother slapped him for not speaking to her in Spanish. Then, before he had a chance to translate for her, she decided she'd understood him well enough. "Mentiras," she hissed. The word meant lies.

"I didn't hit her," the young voice whined defiantly in English. "I threw the grain bag at her."

I was glad to know I didn't have an army of ants marching down my neck, just some harmless columns of oats. The terrier whimpered in my ear and licked it.

"Aiiee, Dios," said the long-suffering mother. She picked up my hand with cool, callused fingers and let it drop. I hadn't expected her to let go. My hand fell, limply, uncontrolled, through a small, silky pile of grain and came to rest on the rough weave of a gunny sack. I couldn't muster the will to open my eyes. My sunglasses rested on the top of my nose. "Aeii, mijo, cariño pendejo, porque hiciste esto?"

While pendejo literally meant a pubic hair, the slang usage translated to something closer to idiot, or dummy. I heard this type of language so often in the kitchen that I understood it even in my groggy state. She'd just asked her dear little dummy why he'd done that.

"She's in red," the boy explained, more respectfully in Spanish. "I thought she was a Northsider. She even has a weird red car."

"Es una gringa!"

My back had been to him, my hair covered by the hood. "Is she dead?" he asked worriedly.

I waited for the answer, half wondering myself.

"No sé."

A boot nudged my rib cage.

"Que vamos a hacer con el cuerpo?"

The boy proposed dumping me in the river.

I forced my eyes open. "Abundio." I meant to shout, but nothing came out, so I tried again.

"Abundio?" the boy said to me. "Do you know Abundio?" He dropped to his knees, his freckled face close to mine.

The mom leaned over my face from the other side, another mass of freckles. I squeezed my eyes shut and then opened them again, but Abundio's friendly, goony face was still there. I'd simply died and been reincarnated when he was twelve. "Abundio?"

The two freckled faces gawked at each other and then back at me. The dampness of the ground was permeating my cotton sweats.

"Emiliano," the boy said.

"Pendejo," the mother hissed. She castigated the boy for having given his name. What if the woman filed a police report?

Now that I was awake, the boy argued back in Spanish that I'd been trespassing.

The mother suddenly brightened. "Mijo, es ella la novia de Abundio?"

The boy shrugged and sighed elaborately. "How should I know?" he asked in Spanish.

Spanish shot from the mother's mouth, rapid-fire, machine gun style, like a Puerto Rican. Children in Mexico didn't speak to their parents the way the boy had. This was what happened when you brought your children to "el norte." She should send him back to the ranch to live with his grandparents.

Emiliano passively bent his head, crossed his wrists and looked bored, the tirade as familiar as Mass.

"Ask her," the mother commanded.

"Ah, Mama," the boy pleaded.

She shoved him and we almost kissed. "Are you Abundio's girlfriend?" he blurted.

I turned my head to empty the grain from my ear and managed to brush my face with a hand. "Yes," I said. "I'm Abundio's girlfriend." This was, no doubt, his mom and brother. For the moment girlfriend status might kindly dispose them towards me. I didn't know how I'd get out of the situation, but it didn't seem wise to underestimate two people who'd calmly discussed dumping my body in the river. "Es poco vieja," she said to her son.

The boy wrinkled his nose with pubescent distaste for the mating ritual.

I smiled stupidly, like I didn't know she'd called me old, and tried to sit. The mother took my hands and easily pulled me up, although I was about eight inches and thirty pounds bigger than she was. The wiry, red-haired lady was only a few years my senior. The thought that if my life had been different, I could have a child as old as Abundio, gave me a strange feeling, mostly thankful, but a bit wistful, too. There was something to be said for having children while young. A woman might be ignorant and inexperienced, but at least she had the energy for the task. At the moment, I felt too old for children, or this kind of escapade. I brushed grain from my sweats and tentatively rolled my head.

"Venga a la casa por un pan dulce." The woman half-closed one green eye and inspected me with a sideways glance from the other.

I used the Mexican's most common defense; I feigned ignorance of the language, and looked, with what I hoped was a convincingly puzzled face, to the boy for a translation.

"Ya wanna have some sweet bread?" he asked, as impatiently as I'd hoped.

She nudged her son. They were so similar in size, that they could have worn one another's clothes, except she seemed strictly a skirt and blouse woman, and the boy wore a Giants cap, an oversized, boldly blocked shirt to his knees, and big jeans. She told him to ask my name.

He complained to her in Spanish. He was supposed to meet Freddy. He didn't have time to spend the afternoon translating for her.

The steely little woman argued back, again threatening to send him back to el rancho in Mexico. After a minute of passionate negotiation, they agreed Emiliano would ask my name, and then, he could meet Freddy.

When Emiliano had done his duty, I lied with appalling dexterity, "Maria."

The mother grinned broadly, Abundio's smile. "Es tan bonita!"

CHAPTER TWENTY-THREE

The police didn't suspect Julieanne or Alexis Fortier. They didn't suspect Victor Medina. They suspected me. I spent the afternoon of New Year's Day in an interview room. I had been summoned.

"Mrs. Sabala . . . ," Detective Carman said over the phone.

"Ms.," I corrected.

He paused, as though making a note of it, but perhaps just irritated.

"Sabala is my maiden name," I explained. "Only Ms. works with that choice." It occurred to me that Esperanza also used her maiden name—Medina. Victor was her brother. It was unusual for a Mexican woman not to take her husband's name and even more unusual not to give a child his name. Could Delores be illegitimate? Esperanza never spoke of a husband or a father.

Detective Carman didn't inquire why I hadn't taken my husband's name, but said, "We'd like you to come down to the Police Station this afternoon for questioning." It wasn't a question, and something about his tone implied if I didn't come to them, they'd come to me.

In a brief fit of paranoia, I wondered if the Medina family had talked to Victor and he had reported yesterday's adventure. I'd watched him and Abundio all morning, but they'd acted the same as always. Victor had even told me a couple of jokes.

I'd wanted to ask him directly if he knew I'd "visited" his house, but I'd been overcome by wimpiness. I had a serious bruise on my head, and had been given the third degree by Chad. He'd wanted, reasonably enough, to know where I'd been all afternoon. I'd heard that the best way to lie was to stick close to the truth.

"I went to Watsonville."

"Why?"

"To visit the Medinas."

He'd narrowed his eyes. "I should have listened to Mary."

That had ended civilized discussion. It had been an unpleasant evening and I simply hadn't felt up to confronting Victor this morning.

I reassured myself that this was the SCPD, not the WPD, and that the Medinas were not about to call the police, anyway.

I dressed in a forest green silk blouse. Donald had told me that was my best color, bringing out the sincere green in my eyes and setting off the auburn in my hair. The color had grown so predominant in my meager wardrobe that I'd invested in dark green pumps. I donned them now below my denim gauchos and inspected myself in the full length mirror on the bedroom wall. "Good," I thought. "How could they suspect me?" I looked thoroughly respectable, a bit like a school teacher, in spite of my bare legs.

I drove cautiously, mindful of road oil loosened and washed up by the recent rains. I tried to reassure myself. I had a telephone relationship with Sergeant Gold. He should remember someone as pesky as me. I took Water Street rather than Soquel Avenue to skirt the maze of detours in the downtown. Unlike downtown Watsonville, downtown Santa Cruz still had a bombed-out, war zone look from the 1989 Loma Prieta Earthquake. I turned left on Center Street and right on Locust to find a spot without a meter. I pulled to the curb along a yard bordered with oleander bushes, battered white and pink petals sprinkled on the damp ground. The irony appealed to me.

As I crossed the street to the old police station, my anxiety increased with each step. I stopped by the white masonry, WPA building, part of the beautifully landscaped block of officialdom. A low stone wall separated the rose garden from the sidewalk. "Come on, Carol," I chided myself. "Buck up. This is a real police interview. The inner workings of a station. You love this stuff," but a small, suppressed, sarcastic voice said, "Sure, in books." I took a deep breath, and forced my conservative pumps to keep moving through the dappled shade as the sun struggled to break free of the overcast. I found myself stepping over cracks.

Even the wire mesh on the windows and the faded police department sign didn't mar the beauty of the long, low building. At the end, an electronic eye circled, watching the entrance and the white and blue cruisers in the lot. The news filmed this building and vandals attacked it, yet, in fact, it housed little of the police department. The building was seriously earthquake damaged, and the heart of the department had moved further up Locust Street to the old telephone company building, an innocuous, ugly, red brick square marked only with a discrete plaque. In spite of my anxiety, I was curious to see its interior. I'd tried to "visit" one day just to see what it was like, only to discover that the front door was locked and one had to speak through an intercom to gain admittance.

I didn't blame the low profile and caution. Police in a liberal town had a tough job. One officer had been under constant attack by a group of women who had accused him of improper searches. Furthermore, police popularity had plummeted thanks to the Rodney King beating.

"Carol," a voice said impatiently.

Making a flank attack down Center Street, my nemesis hobbled toward me in her too-tight shoes. "I've been waving for five minutes."

My thoughts were a string of obscenities. What was I going to tell her? She'd positively relish the idea that I'd been called to the police department. When she reached me, she clasped a hand to her ample breast. Under her nubby yellow jacket, she wore a ruffled, ivory blouse, equally unflattering, but no doubt, an incredible bargain. "Oh my," she panted, "couldn't you hear me?"

Obviously not, I thought, although I managed a nearly civilized, "What's up, Mary?"

"Civic meeting."

This, I suppose, translated to seniors meeting. They usually used the Louden Nelson Center at the other end of the outdoor mall, but with earthquake repair, activities and meetings played musical chairs.

"You're all dolled up," she commented.

I wondered what she wanted. Why did a basically lazy woman gallop a block down the street to see her hated daughter-in-law? Well, of course, she didn't want to see me; she wanted a ride home. And she wanted her friends to be jealous that she seemingly had a young friend. "I can't give you a ride, Mary."

"I don't need a ride," she said airily. "I can call the Lift Line."

Chad, was more like it, I thought.

"I understand how busy your life is."

I sighed in spite of myself.

"I suppose you have an appointment."

"Actually, I do."

Her eyes flicked around for possibilities, and then with her ungodly instinct, she said, "The police department. I told Chad that you'd get in over your head."

It was my turn to lie. "I'm not in trouble. In fact, I'm going down there to give them a tip."

She stared at me as though the truth were a pearl in my black, nasty core. Even though I'd just lied, as a basically honest person, I naively expected others to tell the truth. As a basically dishonest person, Mary was suspicious of everyone, but she blinked heavily in uncertainty. Since I had given the police a tip, I must have sounded convincing.

"Well, then," she said glumly, "I guess I'll just have to sit and wait for the Lift Line."

However, as I continued down Locust, she walked beside me, making me nervous. Fortunately, though, she didn't try to invite herself into the police department.

"Where's the nearest pay phone?"

I shrugged.

"Do you have a quarter?"

This was pure extortion and Mary at her finest. I would have been willing to wager my last ten that if I grabbed her black patent leather purse and shook it upside down, any number of quarters would bounce on the sidewalk. Yet, regardless of the outcome, I'd be the one who'd look, and feel, like an ass. A quarter was a small price to see her back, but it galled me anyway.

I didn't get a chance to see the bull pen or to find Sergeant Gold and hail him like an old friend. I entered a small, distinctly unhomey lobby with offices to the left behind a counter topped with what I imagined to be bullet-proof glass up to the ceiling. Microphones seemed to be the only way to communicate with the rabbit warren of work spaces, but Detective Carmen saved me the trouble by striding through the single door. He directed me to an interview room.

He motioned for me to sit. While no bare light bulb dangled from the ceiling, the room was sufficiently austere with a phony wood grain table, three chairs, bare white walls and metal filing shelves in the corner. I plopped into an upholstered desk chair. Detective Carman sat opposite me in a wooden chair and fiddled with a hand held tape recorder.

"Aren't you going to Mirandize me?" I studied his face and found it handsome, but not as fresh as Chad's or as engaging as Buzz's. It was a face of which I'd tire.

"Let's put it this way," he said. "I invited you to this interview and you came voluntarily. You're here of your own free will and you're also free to leave at any time."

I started to stand, to surprise him, but he wasn't amused. The room felt muggy. Someone didn't realize the air was damp, not cold, and had turned on the heat.

"Okay," I said. My cheekiness dissolved. I sat firmly on the chair.

"After we came to your work yesterday, a witness talked to my partner and told her that you had a book on poisons and that you had talked once about how easy it would be to poison someone."

"Oh, God," I said. That had to have been Patsy. Suzanne would never snitch, but Patsy's first loyalty would be to Detective Peters, a compatriot, a lesbian, although Patsy would use the word queer. She had an incendiary personality that marched the local Queer Nation through the Capitola Mall, and she took seriously her allegiance to the gay community.

I took a deep breath and exhaled slowly. "That is the kind of stuff I like to read. My favorite novel is *Silence of the Lambs* and the niftiest place I've ever visited was the torture museum in the Tower of London. Call me weird, call me odd, call my mom. She'd love the confirmation and commiseration. Furthermore, that book was in an unsecured locker where anybody could have read it." In spite of the big breath, my blood pressure rose and the anger gained momentum. "For that matter, anybody could go to a book store and buy that book."

Detective Carman remained quiet. He may have expected a more docile person, but when I lost my temper, as my mom used to quote, "Fools rush in where angels fear to tread." Or, if I moved my mother to lose her formidable composure, she'd sternly warn, "That temper of yours will get you in trouble someday."

I regretted my outburst. After all, if I were more extroverted, I might have become a homicide dick rather than a baker with a twisted avocation.

"What about the conversation on how easy it would be to kill someone?" Detective Carman asked calmly.

"Yeah," I said defiantly. "We had such a conversation, and I told Patsy poison would be a good way to murder. It's rare, there's no obvious violence, and a homicide investigation often depends upon an aggressive coroner. Don't you agree?"

He gave me a subtle version of the squished-bug look. God, I was beginning to detest the expression. It made me feel like joining Patsy and her radical feminists. If a man discussed poisons or murder, people might consider him knowledgeable or dangerous, but from a woman it was weird and icky. I was tired of being misunderstood by the world because I had a scientific rather than squeamish temperament.

"Anonymous tips help," he said blandly.

The sweat trickling down the inside of my silk blouse felt cold. Did he know?

"Considering that Patsy was my interested audience for *that* conversation, I sure hope you call *her* down for questioning." Something about Patsy niggled the back of my mind, but I knew that I wouldn't retrieve it now, under pressure. Whatever the detail was, it'd surface, unbidden, when I was taking a tray of hot cookies from the oven or making love with my husband.

"She's been here," Detective Carman said flatly.

"What about Julieanne Fortier?" I persisted.

"What about her?" Detective Carman asked. I read the punched labels under the stacks of forms on the metal shelves: Missing Persons, Substance Abuse Report, ... The cop waited patiently until I looked back. His nose looked as though it'd been broken. Normally, I liked that kind of irregularity, but now it bugged me like a bit of bread dough that bubbled instead of baking into a smooth crust. There wasn't anything I could do about it, but the sight still made my fingers itch. I told him the little I knew about Julieanne Fortier.

He explained the term "legitimate suspicion," apparently what they felt about me.

"Jesus," I exploded. "How many homicides are domestic? Her husband is killed; she's the beneficiary of his life insurance, and she disappears. That's not legitimately suspicious?"

"You know a lot." His tone was flat, but the words were full of insinuation.

I lifted my hair to give the back of my neck some air.

"There's something familiar about your voice," he added.

"You've talked to me before," I insisted. Shit, if he'd connected me to the tip line, no wonder I was under suspicion. If oleander had been the poison, who would believe that I'd followed a hunch, made a lucky guess, nothing more? I didn't believe in coincidences; why would the police department? "What about Victor Medina?" I said desperately.

"What about him?" Detective Carman asked.

CHAPTER TWENTY-FOUR

My mom connected my temper to the red highlights in my hair. "You got that red hair from my Grandpa Turner," she'd say. He was dead long before my time, but I'd heard a lot about the legendary figure. My mom had shown me a black and white photo of a huge man with a full beard. "His hair was your color," she'd say, "but that beard was red, red, and we're pretty sure he killed Grandma."

"I wonder if I'd have a red beard," I'd say, rubbing my cheeks (to annoy her, of course). No body had been found, and I liked to believe Grandma Turner had deserted the tyrant, and started a new strain of relatives I didn't know about.

In a decorous way, my mom would discuss her side of the family (at least the ones that were dead), but my father's side remained a mystery. My father had abandoned the family before my memory began. The only thing I loved about him was his name: Geraldo Sabala, although my mom, on the rare occasion when she'd refer to him at all, called him "that poor alcoholic man." My brother Donald had looked vaguely Latino, but my mom was clearly right about the source of my genes.

I thought about this stuff as I took the freeway to Morrissey Avenue, and by the time I got home my Great Grandpa Turner's temper had dissipated.

Our house was an off-white-tending-to-pink stucco affair with a curved path of flat stones to the front door. A palm swept the cloudy sky over the riot of hardy perennials and large rocks. Lola jumped over the redwood fence around the back yard and strutted to greet me, although she kept her tail up and looked around in the air to feign indifference.

"Hello, my sweet Lola," I crooned.

She sauntered past and sniffed at a tangle of invasive Mexican primroses. When I opened the door, the aroma of baking salmon hooked Lola's interest. And mine, too.

"Where have you been, honey?" Chad was cheerful, but concerned.

"I don't want you to call me honey anymore," I said.

He looked dejectedly at our two good Willoware plates set out on the tiny table. He'd hoped for a romantic evening. He was showered and shaved and wearing a blue and black flannel shirt that I liked.

"I don't mean it like that. It's just that every time I hear the word honey, I think of the murder."

Chad circled the freestanding counter and gave me a bear hug. "Poor, poor, poor, poor, baby," he caterwauled in pity. The flannel was soft and comforting.

I joined the chorus. "Poor, poor, poor, poor, baby."

We howled in unison like cats in heat for a full minute and I felt immensely better.

Chad poured us each a glass of dry Chablis and I related my "interview."

"Carol . . . ."

"Please don't give me a lecture," I pleaded.

Chad set an already-prepared green salad on the table and wrapped some of Alfaro's four-seed bread to put in the oven to warm.

He started to open his mouth again. "And please don't say anything about how your mom told you so."

"I won't mention Mary," he said tightly, "if you don't mention Mary."

"This is as good as anything at Archibald's," I said brightly, as we seated ourselves and started eating, "and it doesn't cost twenty-five dollars a plate."

"I thought the Coho looked really fresh," Chad said proudly. "Carol," he began carefully, when my mouth was safely engaged on a challenging hunk of bread. "If there's a link between the honey and the oleander, doesn't that mean someone at work killed Fortier? The person who gave him that present?"

I chewed hard and fast, but finally gave up and talked with my mouth full, a barbaric act. "It looks that way, but I haven't found anyone yet who drew Fortier's name or who received presents from Fortier. Anyone could have left a present for him."

"But wouldn't he be suspicious if he received a gift without being in the exchange?"

"Not Fortier. He had a big ego. He wouldn't have thought twice about a present from a woman, like say Julieanne Fortier, sent into the kitchen via an accomplice."

"Alexis?" he said, disbelievingly.

"Well, she is going to inherit her uncle's condo. That's a motive."

Chad shrugged his broad shoulders.

"And why did Julieanne take off after Fortier's death?"

The collar of his shirt lifted the back of his hair; he was due for a cut. "If she came here to be near Fortier," he speculated, "why would she stay?"

"Her job."

Chad drained his glass. "But what if she thought there would be an investigation, and what if she thought the investigation would expose her role in getting Fortier the program?"

I ruminated on a chunk of bread, and then swallowed the cud. "I'm not sure what her role was in that, but your idea makes some sense, Chad."

He beamed. Maybe he'd get so involved in the puzzle that he'd stop worrying about me.

"I guess I prefer to believe Julieanne did it because it's easier than believing one of my friends did it."

CHAPTER TWENTY-FIVE

The next day while on break, I pored over the chart that I'd made on the back of the old recipe. According to the matching I'd done, if Fortier had received the honey from a Kris Kringle, the person had to be Patsy, Big Red or Esperanza. I didn't feel much like visiting the pastry department after my little "invitation" to police headquarters, but I couldn't let that detour my investigation.

I cruised from the EDR, walked along the loading deck, and entered the kitchen by the walk-in refrigerators. The pneumatic seal on the meat door sucked open. Victor pushed out the door and nearly dropped the Styrofoam chest he was carrying. He stood in a puff of cold air.

The whole scene struck me as odd. "What were you doing in there?"

Victor set down the ice chest, turned his back to me and padlocked the door. "Buzz sent me to get a roast. This seemed like the best way to carry it."

Buzz wasn't supposed to give anyone the key. Maybe that's why Victor seemed surreptitious.

"Don't worry. Your secret is safe with me," I said and continued to the garde manger before I lost my resolve. I stuck my head into the galley.

"Haven't seen much of you," Suzanne sang out.

"Busy, busy, busy," I replied.

"Trying to figure out which one of us is a killer," she retorted good-humoredly.

I put a finger to my lips and walked over to the counter. What had I expected? Nothing stayed a secret in the kitchen. Delores stood over the sink, dutifully peeling carrots.

"I'm amazed we don't have a machine to do that."

She smiled weakly at me.

Suzanne's slim, golden hand wielded a knife the size of a small machete. She pressed a row of bright, exposed carrots to a cutting board with the heel of her hand, the fingers carefully curled. At the rate Suzanne chopped, her fingers could be added to the salad before she even knew they were missing.

"Eldon more or less implied I should back off," I whispered.

"Oh, God. Eldon," she moaned. "What am I going to do, Carol?"

I'd been so preoccupied with my snooping, I'd lost touch with other events in the kitchen. I knew only what any fool could observe. Eldon would let Suzanne's breaks stretch to twenty-five minutes, and never roust her from the EDR. If he looked at his watch when he was near Suzanne, he did so to avert his eyes. He never approached her. She never had to listen to him. And she most certainly had never been written up. It was easy for her to like him.

"I don't like him like that," she protested.

"Like what?"

"God, Carol, you have been out of it. Don't you know about the stuff he gave me for Christmas?"

"Let's go for a beer, Suzanne. Soon. I've gotta hustle. My fifteen minutes are up. Eldon's already been on my case this week."

I'd run out of time again. As I flew up to the pastry department, Patsy gave me a tight, non-smile. I glared at her and suppressed the first-grader instinct to call her a tattletale.

It struck me as one of life's mind teases that she and Esperanza were the toughest women I knew, yet they fussed over spongy petit fours and gooey meringue shells.

"Esperanza," I called.

The woman turned from a tiered cake. She looked like Delores, with flaring cheekbones, full lips and slender nose, but her eyes were brown and the face hardened. She held a paper sleeve full of icing, and baby blue frosting smudged her smock.

"Jes?" she asked automatically.

"Have you had your second break?"

She shook her head.

"Come visit me, okay?"

Waiting for Esperanza, I wiped down the stainless steel counter for the third time. No second shift replaced me. I was the bakery, except for whatever poor fool got stuck in my slot on Friday and Saturday mornings. This week, though, I'd been scheduled for six days in a row. Eldon managed to do that without paying overtime by making sure the sixth day fell into the next pay period. He was sneaky like that.

Esperanza turned the corner, drying her hands on a small, white terry towel. "Sorry, I had to finish tha' cake. Doze pee-pow, the Nichols, have their reception here this afternoon."

Although not more than five or six years older than I, Esperanza seemed of another generation. Perhaps only parenthood caused the shift. Perhaps I'd one day be seventy-six and still relate to teenagers better than to grandmothers. Perhaps the difference was cultural. She had the dignity of an indio mixed with the toughness of a field worker and the style-consciousness of a women's magazine reader, her eyelids painted mauve to plum. America still mystified and frightened her.

"I just have one question," I lied. (I had about a hundred.) "Whose name did you draw for the Kris Kringle?"

She frowned. Although her hands surely had to be dry, she kept wiping them. "I drew Todd for the Kris Kringle." She waited. I didn't want her to leave, but I couldn't formulate a relevant question about Todd. He was a young, curly-haired, back line cook with no apparent motive to kill Fortier, even if he, like every young guy in the restaurant, had a crush on Delores.

"Than' you for the nice presen's, Carol."

"I saw you put one of those glow-in-the-dark Band-Aids on Delores."

She nodded. "I can'd say I'm sad Jean is dead, but I yam worried for Delores. She's so hard-broken."

"You're a good mother."

Drops sprang to the corners of Esperanza's eyes above tri-
angles of purple blusher. This woman did not crumble easily.
Eldon was right. Esperanza was distraught.

"Come on," I said. "I'm off. Let's get out of this place." I laid
my hand on a stiff, but grateful, shoulder.

As we walked by Victor and Abundio, she pitched the towel
into a blue, plastic milk crate. Victor spoke tersely and rapidly to
her in Spanish. As they no doubt intended, I understood only the
tone. It warned.

I didn't get a clue about the murder, at least not any that jumped
up and bit me, but I did learn about Esperanza. She and Juan
Rocha had grown up in Gomez-Farias, a small town near Zamora,
Mexico. Many of the villagers, migrant workers who picked crops,
traveled between Mexico and the Pajaro and Salinas valleys.

After her quinciñera, Esperanza married Juan. The families
had known each other and Juan and Esperanza had grown up
together. Their families wanted them to marry and fortunately,
they were fond of one another.

In the first two years of marriage, Esperanza gave birth to
Guadalupe and Juan. When Esperanza was seventeen, they packed
two plastic bags full of supplies, left the children with Juan's
mother, and used their savings to ride a bus to Tijuana. In the
evening, they walked the brown, barren hills along the border to
La Colonia Libertad.

"Der were a hundred pee-pow in the hills, jus' waiting for
night, so they could run down the hill. All we had to do was
climb a fence and dere was MacDonald's and all the tings of
America."

Esperanza munched apple coffee cake, several days old. "How
do you stay so skinny when you bake so delicious food?" she
asked.

I smiled. "I could ask you the same question." Plus, I thought, she'd borne three children. A person would never know it. Her body was sinewy, her stomach flat, her breasts large and firm.

"Wedding cakes are not delicious." The smooth face relaxed as the brown eyes turned inward, thoughtful, as though considering the metaphoric implications of the statement. "We had tortillas then, and water, but I was so scared I couldn't even eat a tortilla. The helicopters flew over, so low they'd make the dust turn around. I was sure we'd all get caught.

"Someone tol' us to trow away the plastic bags because they were white. Juan wrapped our things in a spare shirt. Someone said to forget the bundles; we'd need to run.

When it got dark, people moved. We did, too. When the spotlight came over, we'd trow ourselves on the floor, or in the bushes. Then some horses came right toward us. Juan dived and rolled but a man on a horse shined a flashlight in my eyes. They handcuffed me and took me with a whole bus load of Mexicans to a deportation camp, like a prison, with wire fence all around. I had a hearing and they sent me back to Tijuana. A lot of people walked right back to the hills to try again. I didn't know what to do. Juan had our money. I had no way to return to Gomez-Farias, so I walked up to the hills, too.

"That night I got across okay. I begged money and lucky I got an operator who could speak e-Spanish. I called Victor in Watsonville. He told me where to go and what to do until he could get me. He hadn't heard from Juan. I never saw Juan again."

CHAPTER TWENTY-SIX

I'd barely shut the door of my Ghia, when a black Harley roared up beside the parked car.

Patsy was decked out in black leather and a law-abiding helmet. She motioned for me to roll down the window.

I didn't mouth, "Fuck off," through the glass, but rather complied, locking her eyes in my steeliest stare. I noted with satisfaction that the motorcycle, now stopped, presented a struggle for her straddled legs.

"I just want you to know that I didn't go to the police to tell on you."

"Oh?" I asked angrily.

"There was some other stuff I thought Sasha should know."

"Sasha?" I asked, with an obnoxious, insinuating flutter of lashes.

"Detective Peters," she clarified, struggling with her incorrigible black beast. "And just for your information, Carol, she's not gay."

I hated knowing that I'd jumped to a wrong conclusion.

The Harley turned a little this way, and then a little that way. "I didn't want Sasha to find out through the investigation about Fortier and me."

"You and Fortier!" I exclaimed in a most impolitic way.

She pulled back her shoulders, offended. "Why not? I have great tits." She sounded sarcastic and angry, deeply angry.

I half expected her to rip open the black leather jacket to prove the merit of her chest. Perhaps she would have if the motorcycle had been less demanding. Something was going on here that I didn't understand.

"You and Fortier had an affair?" I stammered.

She rolled her eyes. "Hardly."

I felt dense for at least the tenth time since I'd gotten involved in this mess. I didn't even know what question to ask.

"Fortier saw me as the ultimate challenge," she said. "He was one of those guys who believes a woman could only be a lesbian because she hasn't met the right man. Namely him."

"He raped you?" I guessed.

She considered the question. "No one but me would think of it that way."

I remembered her bitterness last summer in the sports bar. Yet, I'd never heard a peep about this in the kitchen. Below its surface of dirty jokes and juicy gossip, I glimpsed a black reservoir of secrets. "How was Detective Peters going to find out about this if no one knew?"

"Did I say no one knew?" She fired up the machine and roared off, leaving me to wonder whether she'd simply finished all she had to say, or I'd pissed her off, or she'd tired of fighting the weight of the Harley.

As I watched her vroom down the hill and into the trees, I realized I still didn't know whose name she'd drawn in the Kris Kringle. But, if Fortier had participated, either she or Big Red had gotten his name.

CHAPTER TWENTY-SEVEN

I sat on our brick landing, figuring out what I should do next. Lola circled in the Peruvian lilies, preparing to lie down. She had a section that she'd squashed into a nest. "Get in there and lay some eggs," I told her.

She curled in the long, slender leaves and squeezed her round green eyes shut with either annoyance or pleasure.

I thought about Esperanza's "hijo natural," Delores, born four years after Juan had disappeared. At first, the search for Juan detained Esperanza in Watsonville.

After a couple of months, Victor had suggested, "Maybe the cabron took a hike."

"No. No es posible."

"If we find him able to come, but not here, I'll cut off the puto's cajones."

Across the cafeteria table, the tough little woman had smiled at me. "You understan'?"

I nodded. "You felt Victor would have killed Juan if he'd deserted you."

"Yes," she said, without hesitation. "Yes, he would."

Victor had planted doubt. In Mexico, she and Juan had lived in a carefully crafted vessel, hard as adobe, earthy as patted torti-llas, slow as a paseo. But once they'd scrambled over the fence and Juan's boots thudded on American soil, the vessel and its dreams shattered.

As months passed, Esperanza thought maybe Victor could be right. She stopped looking. Run down and weak, she'd collapsed in an artichoke field. Victor took her to a clinic that diagnosed hepatitis B. After the long illness, poverty chained her to the fields of the Central Coast.

When she'd finally returned to Gomez-Farias, with money for a coyote to smuggle her children, they didn't recognize her. Like Chad, little Guadalupe and Juan had come to know their grandma as Mama. They'd cried and clung at the mere idea that the stranger might take them, and, in the end, Esperanza had returned to the United States alone and broken-hearted.

"You see, Carol, I yam not a good mother."

It was the same conclusion I'd reached about Chad's mom, but given Esperanza's circumstances, the judgment seemed harsh. Maybe if I knew more about Mary, my judgment of her would seem harsh, too. I gritted my teeth and resolved to be more understanding with the woman.

I reached out and absently petted Lola's tail. She gave me one sharp meow and a scathing look.

Esperanza's story made me think Victor, to honor his sister and to protect his niece, might have killed Fortier. I yawned. It was a theory, no better or worse than my theory about Julieanne.

And what about Patsy? No wonder she'd confided in Detective Peters. Patsy had the perfect motivation to murder Fortier. She would have considered killing him environmental cleanup.

She hadn't wanted Detectives Peters and Carman to stumble onto her secret. Better to tell them, especially when she had a sympathetic audience like Detective Peters. She might not be gay, but Patsy had called her Sasha. They must know each other. Patsy's revelation suggested someone else knew about whatever had happened between Patsy and Fortier, someone who had kept his or her mouth shut, but who might now talk. *The flower is pure Patsy.* The niggly detail that I couldn't remember at the police station popped into my head. The petit four that Eldon had said was specifically for Alexis had been decorated by Patsy, but I'd eaten the damned thing instead. I doubted Patsy had shared that tidbit of information with Sasha.

The memory of spewing over the balcony made me retch. I

looked at the contented, brindled ball of fluff in the crushed flowers. "Come on, Lola," I urged. "If the Easter bunny can lay eggs, so
can you."

CHAPTER TWENTY-EIGHT

Mist dampened my face. My feet read the way like braille from the employees' parking lot to the kitchen. The night was moonless and the stars shrouded in fog. Sometimes the night cleaning staff were still around—distant vacuums smothered in fog pillows. This morning I heard nothing—no noisy cart rattling along the sidewalk. In the still, dead air, the eucalyptus leaves didn't rustle. Even my footsteps were muffled.

No light spread itself into the wet air—no late revelers, no early risers, no pacing insomniacs. Three-thirty may have been an obscene time to go to work, but it was a lovely time to be awake, to walk in deep quiet through a seamless velvet. I savored the solitude, the sense of floating as though through outer space.

I walked to the far side of the old novitiate and ascended the steps on to the loading dock, screened from the bricked horseshoe of the main entrance by an island of artful landscaping. The door was locked, but I had my keys in hand, as I always did in the dark. For all my love of the stillness, I was a realist, who carried no purse or wallet and practiced a wary look.

I entered the building, turned left to the poorly lit time clock, and punched in. The brightness of the locker room blinded me. The lights should not have been on, and I felt myself tense, even though occasionally someone did arrive before me, or the last to leave forgot to turn the lights off.

I zipped through a rack of clean uniforms, arranged by size, smocks on one side, pants on the other. I ignored the divisions, and looked for the smock with the prohibited Carol on the inside of the collar in indelible black. Then I began pulling out the pockets of pants to find the one with my name on it. I couldn't shake the creepy feeling that someone was around. My ears felt as though they were rotating back, like an alert cat's, listening for unfamiliar sounds. I'd marked one of the houndstooth checked pants when I'd finally found a uniform that fit. I had a fastidious dislike, anyway, of wearing other people's clothes, laundered or not.

Since no one was around and I wasn't particularly modest, I sat on the bench in front of the lockers, and stripped off my sweats. The one time I'd seen Fortier in his birthday suit, he had been sitting right here, doing just what I was doing, except he apparently didn't wear underwear.

Back then I'd debated a sexual harassment report. I hardly needed to tell anyone, though; Fortier crowed about the situation with special exaggeration of my expression.

Young guys like Todd and Ray were amused. Buzz looked like he'd rip Fortier's head off. Eldon ignored him. Patsy snarled, under her breath, "Fuck with my fluff, and I'll bite your balls off," to which Fortier responded, "Try it, you'll like it." Typical kitchen banter. But maybe the police would see it differently, the way they chose to view my remarks.

I slipped on my uniform. Some people put locks on their lockers, but I operated on the assumption people were about as interested in my ancient, stained sweats, as I was in their clothing. I was fortunate enough to have a top locker and right now the only thing in it was a pair of sturdy, steel-toed, flour-encrusted, size eight work shoes.

As I plopped my sweats and Nike high tops in the locker and pulled out the work shoes, a paper fell to the tile. I opened the sheet of typing paper folded into fourths, and found words cut from a newspaper. The form struck me as a comic anachronism, like a ransom note from a re-run of Perry Mason, a note from someone fearful and naive who believed the local police department had the manpower and wherewithal to track typewriters with flawed keys or with messages still pressed into the platens, someone lacking the anonymity of a computer printer.

The letters jumped around on the page like they must for a dyslexic. They said: STOP SNOOPING. IT WILL ONLY HURT PEOPLE YOU LIKE.

The message was ominous. Until that moment, emotionally, I hadn't believed the murderer walked among us. Now, it was no longer an intellectual exercise. What did it mean about my hurting people I liked? Was this a threat of more violence to come? Or was this the murderer letting me know that he (or she) was dear to me?

As I stepped into the dimly lit hallway, the message was driven home, so to speak, as a figure stepped from the EDR and clobbered me on the head.

CHAPTER TWENTY-NINE

The person who hit me needed a remedial thug course. The blow hurt and stunned me, but it didn't even knock me down. I suppose it did the job. As I grabbed the side of my face, shook my head to clear it, and opened my mouth to scream, the door out of the EDR slammed and footsteps pounded along the loading dock.

I wasn't about to chase someone through folds of clouded night. Especially not in my stockinged feet.

I practiced my mouth a few times to see if it worked. I had the impression I'd been struck with a flashlight, although the idea didn't make sense. The attacker had been too far away. The person had apparently intended to hit me on the back of the head, but a sound had alerted me and I'd turned into the weapon. The object caught me on the jaw, cheek, and upper lip. The lip throbbed. I ran my tongue along it, but didn't taste any blood.

I walked shakily up the hall to the humble employee women's room and inspected myself in the mirror over the sink. The lip was swelling and the skin under my cheekbone was tender to the touch. I'd probably have a bruise there. I peeled up the lip. The inside looked like an overripe plum. It'd be a while before I kissed Chad.

Indignation suffused into the pores of pain. I could understand why someone would murder Fortier, but why would someone from the kitchen slug me? Neither of the blows to my head had been serious, but if my life continued this way, I could end up like Muhammad Ali.

As I crossed down the hall to the EDR, for once in my adult life, I wished my mom were around. Not so she could comfort me, but so she could lecture my assailant.

"You can't beat any sense into her," my mom would say, sadly shaking her grayed head. "She's too perverse. She's been like that since the day she was born." Her bluntly cut, unpainted nails would pick at her knitting. "Why, she wouldn't come out, even when Dr. Kremetz induced labor. Two days later, she changed her mind and didn't even give us time to get into the delivery room . . . ."

I scooped slushy ice from the salad bar trough, wrapped it in a white terry towel bunched on the cold plates, and pressed the compress to my lip. I returned to the locker room to put on my work clogs, which waited patiently for me on the bench as though nothing had happened.

As I made my way up the hall and through the kitchen, I flicked on more lights. I managed to unlock the first refrigerator while still holding ice to my lip. I hated the nuisance of the padlock and wondered, as I entered the cold, how much good it had done in preventing theft. I had a key. Eldon had a key. Buzz had a key. Buzz sent Victor to fetch stuff.

The cluttered disarray of the Use-First shelf had invaded my space. A half dozen new items surrounded the original offending half jar of olives. I had to set down my bucket of coconut macaroon dough and my ice pack to relock the door. I clumsily made my way back to the bakery. I hefted and banged the pail onto my table, wrung the wet towel into the dishwashers' sink, and set the white terry ball on the stainless steel table for future use. Facing the entrance so no one could sneak up on me again, I methodically scooped mounds onto a tray. They looked like heads and I fought the urge to smash them in revenge.

I fantasized that I'd pursued my attacker, tackled him, punched him a retaliating blow in the face, hog-tied him with my kitchen smock and called the police.

Gradually I calmed and thought logically. Who could I trust? Not anyone in the kitchen. Not really. The less I said, the better chance I'd have of staying a step ahead of the killer. I wanted the person to be unsure and nervous, to make a mistake. I'd make him (or her) think I harbored other suspicions.

In the stillness, through my noises and the hum of electric appliances, the door by the refrigerators clicked shut. My heart raced.

I breathed deeply. My internal clock said others should be arriving. Still, I took my rolling pin from the wire racks. Hugging the hallway, I peeked cautiously into the kitchen.

The person whistled "I Saw Mama Kissing Santa Claus." I relaxed. Buzz.

I stood in the open as he rounded the corner by the refrigerator.

He smiled and walked behind the back line toward me. He reached out his arms.

I jumped back.

"Carol?" he said, arching his pale eyebrows into his chef's hat. "What's wrong?"

My mind and heart warred. My heart wanted to let him enfold me while I blurted the whole nasty affair into the warm turn of his neck. My mind said out loud, "What are you doing here so early?"

Annoyance flashed across his blue eyes. "It's not that early, Carol," he said tersely, dropping his hands melodramatically, as though I'd hit them down. "What are you doing wielding a rolling pin and sporting a fat lip?" He mimicked my suspicious tone.

"I'm rolling dough," I lied.

"You are not." He heaved a big, impatient sigh that smelled like vanilla. "You're making coconut macaroons."

"Then none of your business."

"If you say so." He wheeled.

"Well," I said to his back, "you didn't answer my question."

He looked back, the always accessible Buzz.

"Why you're here early?"

"I'm here early because Ray still hasn't mastered lead line." He waited, expecting tit for tat.

"I tripped in the dark."

He tightened and twisted his mouth. "And fell on your lip." He nodded and strode across the kitchen.

As Buzz turned on his steamer, he started to whistle again. It sounded like a funeral march.

I was beginning to relax when Victor leaped around the corner and asked, "Do you know why the pervert crossed the road?"

He smiled in anticipation, combing his wavy black hair with one shy hand. Then he squinted and stretched his bulky neck to get a better look. His brown skin flushed and he touched his own lip involuntarily, asking with his fingers what his Mexican propriety wouldn't allow.

"I fell," I explained.

The hand returned to his hair and I noticed the freshly skinned knuckle. The kind of injury a person might get from hitting someone. Maybe Victor wasn't a clown; maybe he was one fine actor.

"Why did the pervert cross the road?" I asked, amazed at the calmness of my voice.

"He was still attashed to the chicken," he answered, mirthlessly.

He saw my eyes on his knuckles. "I hit something this morning," he said guiltily.

Not "something", I thought angrily. Me.

When Suzanne dropped by, she didn't waste any time. She walked right up to me and said, "Oh my God, your lip."

"I fell." It sounded lamer every time, like mothers who claimed their nearly-maimed children fell down stairs. Suddenly I worried someone might think I was covering up for Chad.

"You iced it?" She picked up the wet towel, and checked its cleanliness. Her golden brown face wrinkled in disapproval to find the bunched cloth empty of cubes. "I'm going to get you more ice."

She strutted off toward the outside icemaker and returned with a bulging, clicking bundle which she thrust commandingly toward me.

I obliged and held the cold pack to my lip. It felt good.

"I was going to ask if you wanted to go for that beer today," she said, looking skeptical.

"It's only a fat lip," I said. "When do you wanna go?"

"How about when I get off?"

"Fine. I'll just hang out and have lunch here."

Since my six days in a row had given me a weekend off, I could take a good, hard look at my suspects. Something about my snooping had upset the killer. Could it have been my visit to Victor's house? Then why had he waited until today? It didn't seem like my questions about the Kringling should worry anyone, unless Fortier had participated and Big Red or Patsy had drawn his name, in which case Fortier would have drawn Big Red or Buzz's name. It was about time I completed that chart, not that it would prove anything. Even if I established that someone had given him the honey as a present, the jar could have been doctored by another person in the kitchen. Why would anyone use a gift traceable to him or herself as a murder weapon? But then again, death row had no shortage of applicants.

I sighed wearily. I needed more little grey cells.

To confuse the killer, at lunch, I asked Alexis for Julieanne's phone number in New Orleans. Let him (or her) think I was going back to my original, corny idea that the wife did it.

Alexis sat in the EDR smashing peas for the simple pleasure of smashing. She would never forgive me for seeing how vulnerable she was. She sniffed her large, French nose and said haughtily, "Oh, Julieanne decided to come back."

CHAPTER THIRTY

Suzanne and I returned to the sports bar where she, Patsy and I had been in the summer. The bartender remembered Suzanne. "Did you come back to watch that cooking show?" he kidded.

Suzanne looked alarmed. "That man, the Cruz'n Cuisine King, is dead."

"Oh." The young man looked crestfallen, not at the news, but at his faux pas. "I owe you a drink," he said to Suzanne.

Suzanne shook her head. "I'm not getting a beer. I want something expensive. A brandy Alexander."

He took her no as a no, and I decided I liked him, even though he had no neck and didn't know I existed. I'd absorbed enough of my mom's Puritanical nature to consider hard liquor in the afternoon decadent. I ordered a Corona with lime.

We waited for our drinks and then took the table farthest from the counter. In order to forestall the subject of my lip, I launched into an account of Chad's jealousy of Buzz, and how I'd grown unsure of Buzz's intentions, lately.

"Don't worry." Suzanne patted my hand. "Buzz is too smart to be that stupid." She pulled off her hair ribbon and slipped it around her wrist. "That didn't sound right. I mean he knows you and Chad are tight." Then she shot me an alarmed look. "Everything is okay with you guys, isn't it? I mean I did notice that you didn't bring Chad to the party."

"Oh yeah, that's fine." I didn't sound very convincing, but it didn't matter. Suzanne had the distracted look of someone who toked too many in the Sixties.

"Speaking of tight," she blushed and looked around, "I've been worried about Buzz, too," she whispered.

"Huh?" I leaned conspiratorially across the table. "Has he been hitting on you?" I tasted jealousy, like a rotten nut.

"He might be blurring the boundaries a bit because he's fallen off the wagon."

I sat stunned, letting the whispered words coalesce into meaning.

Suzanne's hands fluttered in frustration. "I don't mean he'd have to be drunk to come on to you." The nervous hands toyed with her drink glass. She hadn't yet taken a sip. "God, nothing I'm saying is coming out right."

"I didn't take any offense," I assured her. "But why do you think Buzz is drinking?" I tried to sip my Corona, but my fat lip sucked into the opening. I begrudgingly poured it into the glass. "He has a MADD bumper sticker on his car, for Christ's sake."

Suzanne smiled patiently.

"You think Buzz is so insincere? That he'd plaster a message on his car that he doesn't mean?"

Suzanne reached across the table and patted my hand. "I can tell you didn't have any alcoholics in your family."

"Don't condescend to me," I snapped.

Suzanne jerked away her hand.

"Sorry," I mumbled. Apologizing had never been my forte. The guy who gave me the name Sabala, hardly a dad by anyone's standards, had been an alcoholic, but I had no memory of him, so it didn't seem worth mentioning. "I guess you've had some experience?"

"My dad. Believe me, sincerity doesn't have anything to do with it." She snapped her wrist with her scrunchee. "An alcoholic can look you in the eye and say that he won't drink again, and the next day be falling down drunk. And you know what? He was sincere when he said it."

She'd snapped her wrist to a stinging pink. "I still punish myself from time to time," she said ruefully, forcing the punitive finger to become a window washer around her drink's glass. "Remember the Christmas party?"

I nodded.

"Buzz smelled like rum."

"Like eggnog."

"Rum," she insisted. She reluctantly added, "I saw him drinking the kitchen sherry, Carol." She blushed.

I felt ill. Granted that our kitchen used only the finest sherry, not cooking sherry, the action still had the desperate quality of Kitty Dukakis drinking fingernail polish remover. "What did you say?"

"I didn't say anything. I was too embarrassed."

"Does Buzz know that you saw him?"

"I don't think so."

I sighed and looked around the bar—dark wood, lots of beer and sports advertisements, and no ferns. Patsy, Suzanne, and my glib plotting of murder seemed a lifetime ago. At this time of day, the bar was cool and dim. A friend of the bartender sat at the counter and they argued amiably about the Buffalo Bills. Occasionally, the bartender let his eyes slip over to Suzanne.

I thought of Buzz's vanilla breath, and I realized why people use expressions like "heartache" and "heavy heart." Sorrow swelled in my chest until it felt cramped.

"What are we going to do?" Suzanne asked.

I shook my head. "I dunno."

She let silence reign for a while and sipped her drink. "Should I change the subject?" she asked, recapturing some of the Suzanne lightness.

I nodded.

She reviewed the presents Eldon had given her as her Kris Kringle. Some of the things like the truffle and teddy bear had been within reason, but he'd also given her opal earrings and a cashmere sweater.

I remembered Eldon in the mall the night of my own frenzied mission. While I'd never call Suzanne greedy or materialistic, she liked nice things that with our pay she couldn't afford. "Sit back and reap the rewards," I suggested.

"But I feel guilty," she protested.

"Why should you feel guilty if a guy chooses to dote on you? Has Eldon asked you out?"

She nearly shrieked, "Good God, no!"

"Then, what's the problem?"

"I feel like I'm leading him on."

"You're just being gracious. How would he feel if you gave the presents back?"

She snapped her slender wrist with the pale blue band, a sort of self-flagellation for penance. "I know that would be humiliating. And if I embarrassed him like that, what would happen to my job?" She collapsed on to her arms, momentarily folded on the heavy, dark wood of the table, and rolled her eyes up at me. "Oh, God, Carol. What should I do?" She seemed about sixteen.

I didn't feel like much of an advice giver today. If a problem involved just one's self, I could generally decide on a course of action that felt right. But throw in another person, and problems became much more complicated. I did think Suzanne was over-reacting. I wondered if she were a Leo. "I already told you. Relax and enjoy the bennies of having the boss wrapped around your pinky. For all you know, he doesn't want anything but a Platonic relationship."

She straightened. "Now I know you're not taking me seriously. When's the last time you met a guy who gave you a hundred buck's worth of stuff and only wanted to be friends?"

"He could be different."

Suzanne yanked the band from her wrist and screwed her angel food cake face into an expression resembling a withering look. "Eldon *is* different." She jerked up her hair until she looked like a troll doll, then ensnared the curls in the blue band.

She had me there. She sipped her brandy Alexander and delicately licked froth from her pink lips. "Do you think this is sexual harassment?"

"As sexy as your lips are, I don't feel harassed when you lick them."

She smiled briefly and rolled her eyes.

I thought about the question. "I don't know. You don't like Eldon's attention, and it makes your work environment uncomfortable, but you don't have any kind of case if you haven't let him know that."

"Catch 22," she said. "If I tell him, then he might fire me."

"If he does, you have a case."

"Who wants a case?" she moaned.

We sat quietly for a while, trying to see a creative way out of the circle. "Well," I said, "there is the possibility he'll take rejection like a man."

"That's what I'm afraid of."

We laughed.

"Did you know the police came back to Archibald's yesterday?" Suzanne sensed what people did or did not want to discuss, and asked the question tentatively, testing the waters.

"No, I didn't." I'd been so busy dodging queries about my lip, that I'd again lost track of the bigger picture. I tried my beer, but it tasted flat and warm in a glass. "What did they want?"

"It was weird. They went around asking all the same questions you did."

"Like what?"

"You know. Who drew what person and like that. That's why I started worrying again about the Kringle presents Eldon gave me."

I felt both proud and annoyed that the detectives were following my routine. "Do you know who Patsy and Big Red drew?"

She shrugged. "I don't know who Patsy had, but Big Red had Buzz."

I thought about the chart I'd made. If I weren't mistaken, this tidbit left only one, surprising conclusion. "Do you know if the police matched everyone with his Kris Kringle?" I tried to keep my voice nonchalant, while my body vibrated with shots of adrenaline.

"You, for one, were already gone, although I suppose someone knew who you had. Who did you have, anyway?" She drained her glass. The bartender hustled over.

"Want another?"

He didn't check with me, but then, I had a half glass of stale beer in front of me.

"No, thank you," she beamed at him. "I have a pleasant buzz."

The word "buzz" made her face fall, and I felt mine follow suit.

The bartender shifted uncomfortably, probably wondering what gaffe he'd committed now. "Would you like some pretzels?"

"No, thanks. How about you, Carol?"

The bartender looked at me, his eyes dropping to the lip, and then hopping back up.

I felt like screaming, "No, I'm not a battered woman!" but then realized I was. I had been hit, and by someone I knew, too. "No, thanks," I mumbled.

He left.

"That's one thing about having gone with an older man," Suzanne said brightly, trying to cheer me up. "It moves the whole game of seduction to another level."

To hear something positive about a relationship with Fortier disappointed me.

She glanced toward the bartender. "Young guys are so obvious."

Fortier wasn't?

An arm of blue mohair whipped impatiently through the air. "So easy."

"Eldon's older," I teased.

CHAPTER THIRTY-ONE

Soquel Drive followed along the outskirts of Live Oak before descending to the white, steepled church, the picturesque centerpiece to Soquel Village. I told myself that I was taking this route to avoid the rush hour on the freeway, but I also wanted to delay this necessary and overdue confrontation.

I hoped that the Bulldog wasn't home. Ana, the Bulldog, was immense, not big and muscular, but a woman for whom the adjective obese was invented, fat to the point that seats on planes and busses became issues, and issues were what she made of everything from turnstiles to mannequins. Ana's fat body was the center of her universe. She had a one item political agenda. While work needed to be done in the area of women's body images, in a good mood, Ana was gregariously commandeering; in a bad mood she was obnoxiously intimidating.

I turned right off Soquel Drive onto Seacliff and headed toward the ocean. I made a left by a small string of shops, salivating at the sight of Manuel's Restaurant. I hadn't eaten since after work when I was waiting for Suzanne. Even with the car windows up, I could smell the Mexican food through the salty sea air. A quick right brought me to the spruced up beach house.

Real estate agents would call it a "doll house," a pale blue-gray charmer with white shutters and white picket fence. Their front lawn was exceptionally green, the flower borders manicured although nothing was in bloom. Smoke curled from the chimney. I felt bad about disturbing this domestic tranquillity.

Patsy opened the door before I knocked. She was dressed completely in black: thick black socks, black jeans, black sweater pulled over a black turtleneck and her ears dotted with onyx studs, throwing her shock of mauve hair into high relief.

"I didn't know whether you or the police would figure it out first, but I've been expecting a visit."

She gestured me into the living room. The fireplace screen was open and the andirons lay on the hearth, the only items out of place in the room. Ana wasn't on either of the sturdy couches and Patsy looked so pale that my nervousness dissipated.

Aware that this wasn't a social visit, she didn't offer me anything to drink.

"Your lip is sure swollen," she commented tersely, as she perched on the brick hearth and poked at a log. "I guess you know that I drew Fortier's name." She kept her eyes on the fire, and stiffened her voice into a matter of fact statement.

I sat on the edge of one of the blue and white striped couches. "You know, until I completed the chart, I didn't believe he participated."

"You never talked to Ray."

"That's true. But if I remember right he had Delores's name."

Patsy turned. The fire was blazing, but she didn't shut the screen or put up the poker. "Fortier tried to finagle her name from Ray."

I thought about Eldon trading for Suzanne's name and wondered if there was any point of having a drawing in the first place if everyone was going to swap names to get who he or she wanted. Had Buzz traded to get my name? I blushed at the thought. "Well, obviously Ray wouldn't switch."

Patsy smiled grimly. "Yeah, that was cool. Ray's had a crush on Delores since her first day. The only reason Fortier participated was so he could get Delores's name and embarrass her by anonymously giving her a bunch of sex gadgets."

"So why didn't you tell me or the police this?"

"Why? So you'd think I gave him the honey?"

"Did you?"

"What I don't understand, Carol, is why you care who killed

him. The person did the world a favor."

"I guess it has to do with truth, justice and the American way," I said lightly, so she could take it as a joke if she wanted. "So, did you kill him?"

"No." She turned and gave the log a vicious poke. It tumbled from its stand into the corner of the fireplace, shooting up embers. Patsy jumped. "Fuck!"

The agitated woman lifted the poker. I hopped up from the couch. Not again, I thought. I did not want to get hit twice in one day.

My imagination was in overdrive. Patsy put the poker in its stand and picked up the tongs. She busied herself with maneuvering the log back into place.

"Well, if you didn't give him the honey, what did you give him, Patsy?"

She laughed bitterly and twisted around to look at me. "At the time I thought it was funny," Patsy said. "But in retrospect, I can see it was just mean spirited. Like the syrup of ipecac that I put in that petit four."

I deduced that one person had known about Fortier and Patsy and that had been Alexis. But she was right about the mean spiritedness. I got really sick from that petit four. Even if Alexis had blindly sided with her uncle, even if she'd lorded her uncle's power over Patsy, she didn't deserve the treatment I'd received. The girl was hardly more than a teenager. She was entitled to a degree of misplaced loyalty and obnoxious behavior, survival techniques until she could become more of an adult.

Remorse softened Patsy's strong face. "I was as bad as Fortier. That's part of the reason I didn't want anyone to know. I feel like the grinch. I didn't give the son-of-a-bitch anything."

CHAPTER THIRTY-TWO

Kicking wrinkles from the extension, I dragged the phone from the bedroom and sat it on the small table. I made a second trip for the phone book.

I plopped on the wooden chair and watched Lola through the sliding glass door. She hunched, peering through the dusk at movement under the lantana. I turned to the yellow pages and found a beekeeper supply store in San Jose. It wasn't quite 5:30. Even if they'd already closed, someone might still be there to answer the phone. I dialed.

A pleasant, older-sounding woman answered.

"I was wondering if you could tell me how far bees travel for food?"

"They'll travel a long ways, sometimes miles, to forage. That's why, if a beekeeper wants to label his product clover honey, clover has to be the primary foliage for a two-mile radius."

"Thank you," I said. "I think that answers my question."

It seemed unlikely that Victor, or anyone, could control bees enough to produce a reliably poisonous product. That would involve a painstaking effort. A long term, obsessive plot. Fortier's murder didn't have that feel.

Some mysterious person had given Fortier a jar of honey that anyone could have doctored.

On the other hand, Victor was the one with the scraped knuckles after my attack. He raised bees and hated Fortier. But, would a guilty person flaunt incriminating evidence? He could have worn a bandage and said he had a cut or burn, such a common thing in the kitchen that no one would have thought twice.

Lola sprang into the bush.

I tried to think of a good story to explain my lip to Chad. If I told him the truth, he'd become paranoid about my safety, when there wasn't much danger. If the person had wanted to kill me, he could have easily done so. I believed the person, at most, wanted to scare me. Or, the person may have just delivered the note and been interrupted, hitting me out of fear.

I thought about once when I'd wrenched a weed from the ground. It turned out not to be a weed at all, but a shoot from a tree. I'd strained with all my might until the growth suddenly snapped and my hands, clutching a long, green strand of leaves, flew back and blackened my eye. I could tell Chad something like that.

I told him the whole truth and nothing but the truth. He took a pack of Camels from his beat-up Levi's jacket and shook one out right in front of me.

"Chad!"

He opened the glass door, stepped out onto the bricks, and like a one-handed expert, struck a match and lit the cigarette. Dusky, cold air rushed into the house. "If you don't want me to smoke, don't tell me shit like this."

"Well, I considered lying."

"That's not what I mean."

"To me what you mean is I can be held accountable for *your* smoking. That pisses me off, Chad."

Chad turned around and exhaled smoke in a thin, angry jet. "Don't be such a hypocrite, Carol. If you don't want me to endanger my life, why should I let you endanger yours?"

"My life is not endangered," I stated stubbornly.

He licked his fingers, pinched out the cigarette, and put the unsmoked portion back in the pack. "Who's in denial here?"

"You're twisting everything, Chad."

He stalked into the kitchen, barely calmed by the tokes of nicotine. "Then let me make *my* meaning clear. Tomorrow I want you to go down to the police station. I want you to report what happened. And, I want you to stop poking around in this murder before you get really hurt."

"Are you telling me what to do?"

"Am I stupid?" He managed a faint smile. "I am merely, for once in my life, Carol, telling you what I want."

CHAPTER THIRTY-THREE

Chad was long gone when I opened my eyes. He liked working in the winter. In spite of the increased danger from dampness, the roofs were cooler and work was limited by the shortened daylight. He had a laid back nature, lacking my puritanical drive.

My mother had made the patchwork quilt resting on top of me. I contemplated it lazily and thought if one wanted to get literary, it might symbolize our relationship. All manner of sizes and shapes had been hastily machine sewn with no discernible pattern and the corners puckered. My mom had inherited more of her Grandpa Turner's impatience than she'd ever admit. Yet, the quilt had so clearly been made for me with deep, forest green and dusty rose the predominant colors, a little gold for dazzle, and a ruddy brown to stabilize the menagerie. Another blanket, probably faded or worn, had been inserted in the middle to give the quilt weight and warmth, and also, in my mom's typically frugal way, to save the old blanket. Durable, but soft flannel backed the quilt.

It was ugly and I'd never buy it, but if the house caught fire, I'd dash through flames to rescue it.

I stretched one foot, then the other, feeling the cramped bow of the arches. I touched my rubbery lip and wondered if collagen produced the same weird, stretched smooth texture. If it did, how did models deal with having their lips feel like beach balls?

Lola padded up from the foot of the bed and meowed in my face.

"Oh, poor Lola," I whimpered. "Neglected and starving."

I closed my eyes.

Lola reached out a paw, unsheathed one claw, and poked my hand with it.

"No!" I barked.

She sprang from the bed, walked indignantly to the living room, and scratched the couch.

I leapt out of bed. "Stop that, Lola!"

She fled under the table. She had me up. Now she just had to get the hand to reach under the cupboard, to grab a fistful of IAMS, and to throw the crunchy nuggets into the bowl.

She peeked around the table leg, widened her green eyes, and meowed once, as piteously as possible.

I refused to be manipulated by a cat. I held up a spray bottle full of water. "See this, Lola?"

She shrank behind the leg of the table.

"I'm going back to bed and I'm taking this with me."

I stomped to the bedroom, set the bottle on the stand, and hopped back into the delicious warmth.

I did not look forward to humbling myself to crooked-nose Carman. I considered Chad's request reasonable, but I didn't want to do it. This was the kind of situation where marriage got tricky.

Lola hopped on the bed, sauntered up my body to my chest, and peered into my face.

I snaked one hand into the cold and scratched her spotted ear. "Such faith in my goodness and restraint."

She purred, circled, crushed a boob, lay, and began to bathe.

My pleasures were simple. I loved lying in a warm bed with a happy cat on my belly.

I wrangled with my conscience and reached this compromise. I'd go to the Police Department, but I wouldn't make an appointment. If no one could see me, too bad. I could look Chad in his aquamarine eyes, throw up my hands, and protest, "I tried."

I had the weekend off, a rare opportunity, and I planned to take advantage of it, maybe see what Julieanne Fortier was up to these days.

Chad's request that I stop investigating had to return to the bargaining table. I'd tell him that I understood his concern, but there were things I had to do to be me, dangerous or not. If he argued, I'd remind him of my support for his bungee jumping escapade, a seventy-dollar expense for a completely nonsensical, one-minute thrill.

He'd claim it wasn't dangerous.

Simultaneously, I planned my argument and a visit to Alexis and Julieanne.

CHAPTER THIRTY-FOUR

Julieanne and Alexis Fortier lived off Capitola Road in a sudden apartment development, four boxy buildings that heaved, brown and stark from a field, the parking lots fresh, tarry insults to nature, the intimidated landscaping still recovering from shock. Ten years ago the Live Oak area of Santa Cruz had narrow roads through spacious lots, grazing pastures, and large vegetable gardens. Now the sometimes tastefully designed, but always cheaply constructed, monstrosities erupted everywhere and cast long shadows over the original bungalows and farm houses.

Alexis and Julieanne lived in the back building, on the back side, facing the San Lorenzo Creek. I climbed concrete steps, the free standing kind that reverberate, to a small concrete landing with an orange door to my right and to my left.

I rang the bell for the door on my left. When it opened, a miasma of smells sweated from the room like oily heat waves from a busy highway. Julieanne Fortier stood in the palpable stench wearing a dirty, blue, knee-length terry robe. Curlers dangled from her hair. I didn't know anyone still used them.

She scowled, making uglier the tear-soaked, alcohol-bloated face, exhaling cigarette breath. "I don't want any."

"I'm a friend of Jean's," I lied before she could close the door. She narrowed her eyes.

"A co-worker," I amended.

"Oh, yeah," she said. "I remember you from the funeral." She backed up a step and yanked curlers from her hair. "Wanna come in?"

That was grounds for philosophical debate, although my mom

would say without equivocation, "Of course you wanted to enter. You can tell what a person wants to do by what he does."

Julieanne had the house closed up, all shades and curtains drawn. As my eyes made out my surroundings, the swampy smell separated into its components: whiskey, Kool cigarettes, menstruation, the glue and newness of the nubby, dark blue carpet, and the pizza box and coffee grounds in the overflowing garbage can at the end of a counter. This sloppiness didn't go with my impression of compact and spry Alexis, but I had no problem pinning it on Julieanne, now slouched and spreading on the couch. Against the backdrop of muted stripes of color, Julieanne picked at her eyes' crusties, and then combed her hair with the hand.

I sat away from her, on a wooden stool pulled up to the kitchen counter. Without any embarrassment, the woman poked through a heap of elbows in the ashtray, straightened the most-promising, and lit the crooked third of a cigarette.

"Rough time," I said ambiguously.

"Jean's death unhinged me," she stated, quite matter-of-factly for an unhinged person.

"Why did you return to Santa Cruz?"

She exhaled slowly, a leisurely and sensual act. "When I got back to New Orleans, it heightened the fact Jean was gone. We courted there and married there. His family's there and like me, they've never recognized the separation. Good Catholics." She bent the butt of the finished cigarette—her trademark. "But here in Santa Cruz, Jean never belonged to me. Not really," she said wistfully. "He never needed to divorce me. I let him have whatever he wanted."

For a moment I thought she'd cry, but she finished strongly. "Anyway, I got to New Orleans and said, 'What am I doing here? I don't have a job. I like Santa Cruz better and Alexis is like a daughter to me.'"

More like a mother, I thought. "Do you have a job here?" I asked.

"Well, no." She seemed surprised by my question, pulled her

robe more securely around her and peered longingly at the mound of butts.

"I guess you quit your job at KRUZ t.v.?"

The mind, numbed by alcohol, tears, and self-pity, slowly sensed I had not come to offer condolences. "That's right."

"Why?"

Suddenly she didn't care about her hair or whether the robe pulled apart to reveal ample cleavage. She stalked past me to the kitchen, poured herself a half glass of Jack Daniels, straight up, and took a chest-burning gulp. She coughed. "Who are you?" she asked in a strangled voice.

"Carol Sabala."

She coughed several more times, pounded her chest, and then took another slug as though that might help. Tears sprang to her eyes now, but they weren't from grief. "I mean who are you?"

I sank momentarily into a metaphysical quandary, unable to speak. Where did one start—a baker, a thirty-three-year-old, somewhat-liberated female married to a roofer named Chad, daughter of Geraldo and Bea Sabala . . . .

I avoided the imponderable with resumed offense. "Did you quit because of the mess Fortier got you into? Were you afraid the murder investigation would reveal how you and Fortier screwed Buzz Fraser?"

"Jean Alcee didn't get me into any mess," she snarled. She slammed the glass onto the counter and slung her arms across her formidable chest.

"Do you mean it was your idea?"

"No," she snapped. "What I mean is I'd happily do anything for Jean Alcee."

There were two options. She was lying. Or, she meant it. I'd met people like that who wouldn't take responsibility for living, but stuck to others like cockleburs and rode through life on the blind side of a leg. These people scared me.

"Did you kill him?" I asked.

She looked mystified. "Jean Alcee didn't want to die."

CHAPTER THIRTY-FIVE

No matter how snotty I got, Detective Carman maintained a professionalism designed to incite madness.

I cursed my bad luck—that he'd been there, that he'd been eager to see me, that I was back in the humid room. My underarms steamed crescent moons into my gray turtleneck.

I'd dutifully reported the whole episode of the fat lip, resenting every minute of it.

He'd suggested politely that I back off, to which I'd suggested snottily that the police feared the competition.

"Not because we're afraid you'll undermine our investigation," he responded, keeping his cool, "but for your safety."

"You don't think ordinary citizens can solve crimes?"

He sighed wearily and pushed the report form across the table, indicating with his index finger where I should sign. "You have nice hands for a policeman."

"We're saying this for your protection," he said. "We have no doubts about your ability to scare the perpetrator. After all, he assaulted you."

"So, what you doubt is my ability to protect myself?"

He refused to be baited. A long, articulated finger capped with a neatly, manicured nail, tapped the paper. "Let's put it this way, if I were you, I wouldn't eat anything at work."

Even though sweating under my heavy hair, my neck still prickled at Carman's words. "You said 'he.' Do you think my assailant was a man?"

Carman sat sphinx-like, waiting for my signature.

"A friend of mine said you returned to Archibald's and asked about the Kris Kringle. Do you think it's important?"

He leaned back in his chair. He shook his head.

"No?" I probed.

"That shake means you're impossible."

"My mom would agree. But, if I were a man, you'd both call me determined."

He glanced at the still unsigned report and wiped his forehead with his shirt cuff. His dark hair looked damp at the tips. Since he was obviously hot, I wondered if the room were overheated on purpose. "To be honest, we don't have the time or energy to pursue an obstruction of justice case."

"Obstructing justice? Me?"

He rubbed his chin thoughtfully. "If you withhold information."

"All I have are theories, and I tried to share those with you before."

"You mean the Julieanne Fortier idea?"

"That was one."

"Was?"

"I went to see Julieanne Fortier today and eliminated that possibility," I confessed.

"Eliminated? How?"

"Julieanne would have blown Fortier's brains out if he'd asked her, but I sincerely doubt he requested her to put oleander in his honey, so I don't think she did it."

"Oh," he said, with a twitch of a smile, "solid evidence."

I looked down as though reading the report and a trickle of sweat rolled to the front of my neck.

"We could view that as tipping off a suspect."

"Alexis is my co-worker. I have a right to visit her if I want."

"Alexis is at work," he said.

For all Carman's skepticism of my instinct, it registered with the sensitivity of a new lover's lip the promptness of his reply and the timbre of his voice. "You keep awfully good track of the people in this case."

His hesitance was the kiss of certainty.

"So you and Alexis . . . ." I fluttered my fingers and smirked. I could picture them together. Although Alexis was petite and Carman average-sized, they both had compact bodies, large brown eyes, and humped noses, Alexis' by nature and Carman's most likely by a fist. They'd age into look alikes. I could imagine them wearing matching shirts and walking hand in hand at the mall. "Fortier left Alexis a nice condo," I teased. "Maybe the two of you plotted the whole thing."

"I met Alexis on this case," he said seriously. "I haven't asked her out, nor will I until the case is concluded."

He was so forthright that I felt ashamed of my prying. I certainly didn't want to discourage him. Alexis needed someone to distract her from the hopeless crush on Buzz. "Can't we work together?"

"My question exactly."

We sat across from each other locked in a childhood stare down. I'd honed the skill with my mother and it came back to me in an instant.

He blinked first. "What do you want?"

"If you tell me one thing, I'll sign this and then we can both get out of this steam bath."

"That's extortion."

"And I'm a bitch. But if I were a man, this would be negotiating and I'd be called tough."

Carman didn't agree or disagree to the deal.

"Did you ever find the honey?" I asked.

"Isn't that obvious?"

CHAPTER THIRTY-SIX

On my second day off, housework became unavoidable. As I pushed our oiled dust mop around the oak floors, my mind meandered through motives.

Buzz had the best one. Revenge for stealing the show. And maybe more if Fortier had discovered that Buzz had started drinking again, and had used that against him. Fortier's death had not only eliminated any future threats, but also positioned Buzz for a move into management, not that Buzz would have any interest in management. He wasn't that concerned about money. He liked to cook. Revenge, pure and simple, would be his motive.

Dust balls and cat hair collected before the gray ropes of the mop. I swept through a column of ants, marching toward Lola's dish and forecasting rain, then pushed the mess onto the piece of cardboard Chad and I kept behind the refrigerator. It worked better than our dustpan. I placed Lola's bowl in a dish of shallow water to create a moat. I shook the mop out the back door and put it in the closet.

From our towel and rag drawer, I extracted a piece of terry cloth, part of my last bathrobe, dotted it with lemon oil, and started the most boring, and therefore the most seriously neglected task—dusting.

A whole chain of people had advanced because of Fortier's death, but that didn't seem like a strong enough motive since we all received abysmally low wages.

After the first windowsill, my dust cloth was black, but I didn't fold it yet, as the others were just as grimy. I'd never considered Suzanne a spurned lover until the day before yesterday. She might have been more jealous of Delores than any of us dreamed.

The truth was I found revenge and ambition better motives because I understood them better. Jealousy mystified me. I'd long ago decided if a person didn't like me, that was his problem, and if he liked someone else better, that was his prerogative. Competing for a man's affections seemed such a waste of energy.

Another possibility was money. Maybe Alexis had killed him for the condo. I wondered what Carman thought. He hadn't asked her out yet, but that could be out of professionalism, as he claimed, rather than any real suspicion.

Now that I'd finished windowsills, I folded the cloth to a fresh spot for the furniture and realized I should have started with the cleanest stuff first. That showed how little expertise I had at housework. I felt equally as clumsy and illogical with my investigation.

I kicked myself for wasting time on the Kris Kringle. Even with all the givers and recipients matched, the fact remained that anyone could have given Fortier the honey, including Alexis.

I hated to throw away a good rag, but every fold was now black with grime. I filled a gallon jug with Miracle Gro and water and made the rounds of my neglected plants.

There was the possibility of a jealous Delores. My guess was that the police had never found the jar of honey. Maybe Delores had fabricated it. A distraction. No, the present to Fortier had been mentioned by Eldon. Well, how about the protective uncle, who not only raised bees but had scratches on his hand, or a protective mother . . . .

I needed to find out more about her "hija natural." A weird thought tapped at my mind. What if Fortier had had his fling with Esperanza nineteen or twenty years ago. I tried to dismiss it. Certainly he'd know if he'd gotten Esperanza pregnant. I couldn't believe Fortier would make a play for his own daughter. Yet, I knew such ugliness existed. I didn't have to look any farther than what had happened to Chad.

The phone rang. "Hello." Silence greeted me and I guessed at the caller. "Mary? Hello, Mary?"

"Isn't Chad there?"

"He had a job this morning." I wondered why she would have thought he'd be home. Perhaps Chad had given her that idea or maybe she was simply confused.

"Well, would you please deliver this message to him?" the long-suffering voice began. "I thought he'd be home. Tell him that I had to go to the Social Security office because they're saying I've been using the wrong number . . . ."

The woman would have needed to moan to sound more self-pitying. I felt fury bubbling up in me. Here was this woman who'd abandoned her baby, left him with her parents. Granted she had divorced her alcoholic husband and already had a twelve-year-old boy to support, but it's not as though she'd settled down to that task. Instead she'd tried on men like suits of clothes, until finally after about ten years she remarried to a man who turned out to be worse than her first.

". . . and then after I do that, I'm going to have to ride the bus all the way out to Emeline . . . ."

"Mary, I don't know when I'm going to see him."

"But you will tell him, won't you, that . . . ."

I seethed. What claim did Mary have to Chad's devotion? After marrying her second jerk, she'd retaken custody of Chad who was already eleven years old. They had no control over the older boy Ashley, a grown hoodlum. He did nothing. When they tired of his sponging, Ashley stole what he needed. He resented Chad. Chad, on the other hand, had longed for his grandparents. Only when Ashley beat him, blackened both eyes, broke his left arm, cracked a rib, and left contusions up and down his legs, only when Chad was taken to the hospital and Child Protective Services got involved, only then did he get to return to his grandparents.

The stuff Mary griped about constituted the mainstay of her life, but she talked as though she were being singled out and intentionally harassed. I stifled the urge to tell her these were her problems or that I'd refuse to tell Chad. Chad would not appreciate it. And that's what I hated most of all. In spite of her neglect and irresponsibility, he loved her.

"I'll tell him." I sounded nearly as martyred as she did. Chad would, however, get an edited version. I was not about to guilt trip Chad for her.

After the call, I sat on the back steps and did some serious thinking about murder. To be more honest, I pictured me and Mary in the kitchen. I had a frying pan in hand. Mary pushed my buttons, the Turner temper blazed, and KAPOW. The scene didn't even strain my imagination.

But the crime at Archibald's hadn't been done in a fury. It'd been planned. I imagined collecting some oleander. Easy enough. There was a bush of it at the corner of our street. I could see myself boiling it into a syrup and mixing the potent poison in some honey, but I couldn't see myself actually giving it to Mary. Whoever had killed Fortier must have really hated him.

CHAPTER THIRTY-SEVEN

Chad unlaced and pulled off his boots. His body sank deeper and deeper into the couch. He reached for the remote.

Later I'd casually say, "Oh, by the way, Mary called." If I told him now, he'd jump up to return the call, even though the very act testified that she was safely home. For the moment, I wanted him to be mine.

Chad flicked restlessly through the channels, stopping on the local news. Unlike me, he didn't mind if someone talked while he watched television. He didn't become engrossed; often he had to switch back and forth between programs to generate enough interest and action to hold his attention, a habit either conducive to or indicative of schizophrenia.

"Chad," I said in my most buttery voice. I curled beside him and put a hand on his thigh.

His head whipped around. He eyed me suspiciously. He expected me to confess that I hadn't really visited the police yesterday. He couldn't believe that I'd done what he wanted, and he knew me too well to think that I'd complied fully.

I met his eyes and held his hand. I'd mastered stare downs by age ten, and kept the skill honed by practicing on Lola. His face gradually changed like a composite sketch as information was added. The eyes mottled with hurt, worry, and guilt. He loved me too much to force me to change, in spite of his concern. I wondered if this meant he loved me more than I loved him, since I had no intention of giving up my stop smoking campaign.

Chad gave me a small, chagrined smile. "So, what's up?"

"A new angle."

He sighed deeply, but didn't protest. He'd already known there would be one, and accepted it. He flicked through the channels.

Hungry for a trustworthy audience, I spewed my latest idea about Fortier, Esperanza, and Delores.

"You think Fortier is sleeping with his own daughter?" His incredulous, grossed-out voice churned up all my doubt. "Just to get revenge on Esperanza?"

"Not really," I said lamely. I pushed to the other side of the couch to pout. "But then, I don't think anyone would sleep with his daughter, but guys do."

"Well, Delores isn't Fortier's daughter."

"How do you know?" I sounded snotty. Chad's tight lips, hurt eyes, and flurry of channel surfing reminded me that he was barely tolerating this.

"You're forgetting basic, high school biology."

He sounded condescending.

"Enlighten me."

I sounded sarcastic.

"Delores is a blue-eyed babe."

For all my pontificating about jealousy, ice cold needles stabbed my heart. Chad didn't call women babes.

"Esperanza's Mexican and Fortier's French, right?"

"Both brown-eyed," I confirmed, pulling out of my funk and letting logic sink in.

"So it's impossible," Chad said.

"Is it?"

He sighed in deep exasperation.

"Well," I persisted, "is it? Aren't there throwbacks?"

"Carol, I'm ninety-nine point nine percent sure it's impossible."

"That still leaves one chance in a thousand. Better odds than the lottery."

CHAPTER THIRTY-EIGHT

On a small square of waxed paper in the center of the stainless steel bakery table, creamy caramel rolled down from the white stick plunged into an apple's heart. Around the stick, the rich brown had thinned to reveal a circle of green, most likely the crisp tartness of a Granny Smith. The caramel, collected on the waxed square, beckoned to my finger. While I didn't feel like eating a whole carameled apple for breakfast, I could scarcely resist a sample, and Carman's words haunted me: "I wouldn't eat anything at work." Scarier still, the person who'd put the apple on the table knew me well, knew that working in the bakery, I was immune to the temptations of cookies, muffins and pastries. I liked bread only if someone else baked it. However, I loved the crunch and taste of carameled apples.

I pulled out the two-foot rolling pin and whacked the apple as though it were a rat. I felt like the comedian Gallagher, smashing food. I detested that part of his act in the same way the food fight in *Animal House* offended me. Only in a well-fed, pampered culture, I thought. I felt shaken, paranoid, and guilty as I wiped up the smashed bits of apple with a white towel and shook them into the fresh, blue plastic liner of the garbage can. I threw the towel in the wash, cleaned and stashed the rolling pin, and lathered my hands with soap. I fought tears. This whole thing was getting to me. I was not cut out to be a detective.

As I collected my wits and headed to the cooler for my dough, I heard a whistled rendition of "Jingle Bell Rock."

I wanted to bolt to the phone in the hall, to call Chad, and to keep him talking for the next hour until someone else got to work. My stubborn, stupid streak rooted me as the whistling grew louder and louder.

Buzz came out of the back hallway and beamed at me.

"Christmas is over!" I snapped.

He stopped whistling. He stopped walking. He carefully sat down the tray he'd been balancing on the prongs of a hand.

"Carol?" he said softly from across the room. "Tell me what's wrong."

"That apple. You left me that apple."

"Yes," he confessed. "I thought you loved carameled apples."

"Why?"

Like a pubescent boy, he looked down. He wore steel-toed work shoes. From across the kitchen, I could see the blush crawl up his fair neck. "I like you."

"You can't like me," I stammered. "I'm married." I moved my arms like an adamant umpire calling safe. "Forget it."

"I respect that, Carol," he said so quietly I barely heard him. "It doesn't stop how I feel."

I felt stupid to my toes. My eyes stung with frustration. I'd possibly made an egregious error and humiliated my favorite person in the kitchen. "Why'd you give me that apple?"

We stayed frozen on opposite sides of the kitchen. Since I'd already asked Buzz that question, he mulled over alternate responses.

"I gave you the apple to make up after the other day. I felt bad that I'd pushed you to tell me about your lip. That's the kind of thing a person has to be ready to talk about."

"Chad didn't hit me," I blurted.

"I didn't think he did," Buzz replied quickly.

Perhaps he'd thought Chad and I were on the fritz. What better time to make a move? Or perhaps he'd killed Fortier and had now given me a special treat injected with arsenic. Perhaps he was drinking again, and had lost a firm grip on reality. Perhaps, he was the kind, gentle soul I'd always thought, trying hard to cheer up a friend who'd been behaving in a strange way.

This scene sucked, but at least I knew what I had to do.

CHAPTER THIRTY-NINE

Without getting my dough, I turned back to the bakery. I took the dirtied towel from the wash and gingerly pinched smashed apple from the clean, garbage can liner.

I felt his presence behind me and whirled. Buzz blocked the doorway.

My heart hammered.

He stared at the apple fragments in the white terry.

"New recipe?" he inquired with a sardonic smile and the lift of one blond brow.

"Cobbled apple," came the riposte from some altered state while my conscious mind scrambled to decide whether Buzz Fraser meant to kill me. If he drank our kitchen sherry on the sly, and apparently he did, I didn't know him, and I didn't know what he was capable of, except masterful deception. Behind me lay the rolling pin. Just a couple of steps and an arm's reach.

Buzz stepped into the room. "Are you afraid of me, Carol?"

I nodded. Buzz was not dumb. My fingers trembled as they folded the towel around my evidence. Forensics could conclude my doubts.

"You think I killed Fortier?"

I decided then if he weren't guilty, nothing would happen if I reached for the rolling pin, and if he were guilty, I needed an equalizer. I bounded and stretched. So did Buzz.

As I jerked down the rolling pin, he caught my wrist, but I continued the momentum with my whole body and the wooden roller slammed into his thigh with reassuring solidity.

"Jesus Christ, Carol!" he yelped, but not loosening the manacle on my wrist. "I knew you were going to do that!"

I kicked at his shins, but he jumped back, the grip on my wrist plunging me forward. I heaved around my left and hit him on the side of the face hard enough to hurt my fist.

"Let go of the goddamn rolling pin, Carol!"

He grabbed for my free hand, but I hopped back and kicked at him.

He stuck a foot behind my leg, tripped me, and caught me as I fell. He stumbled after me on to the floor, sprawled over my body, and pinned me to the tile. He panted. His chef's hat had fallen off and his fine hair puffed in various directions.

I bucked and twisted.

"Stop it, Carol."

"You stop."

"I will when I know you don't intend to hurt me."

"Me hurt you?" I said angrily, thinking about ways to inflict great bodily damage.

"You don't think I'd hurt you? Do you?" he asked incredulously. The cornflower eyes pored over my face, searched my eyes. "I didn't kill Fortier, Carol. And I'd never, never hurt you."

"You're hurting me now."

He released my arms. I could have bashed his head with the rolling pin, but I'd decided he was telling the truth.

"Why did you follow me in here?"

His hand reached for my hair. Instinctively, I jerked away.

"Because I couldn't stand having you shut me out." The large fingers caressed my cheek, gently stroked my hair. "I've cared about you for years, Carol. But it seems like ever since Christmas, ever since you figured it out, you've felt compelled to treat me like shit."

"I thought you poisoned that apple to kill me."

Buzz shook his head. Still straddling my lap, he reached up to the table and pulled down the white terry package. He opened the towel and stuffed bits of apple into his mouth.

I panicked. "No! No! Spit it out, Buzz! Spit it out!"

For some reason he did as I commanded and secreted his

mouthful into the towel as delicately as an Archibald's customer might dispose of an olive pit. His eyes roamed over my face. He spread over me, my body sandwiched between cool ceramic and warm muscle. I thought a thousand things, but my lips had a mind of their own.

It was the saddest kiss of my life. Beyond the tender lips and the breath mint, I could taste it, the fumes rising to the recesses of his mouth from the high octane pool in his stomach.

CHAPTER FORTY

"What are you doing!" Victor exclaimed.

Buzz and I untangled and stood. Victor didn't wait for an answer to what we were doing. He rolled his eyes and beat a retreat to the storage room. Usually Victor moved stealthily, loading stacks of plates, and heavy rubber honey-combs of cups and glasses onto a cart. This morning everything rattled and jingled and thumped.

Buzz and I stared at each other. I felt flushed. He was an excellent kisser. I brushed bits of grit from the forearms of his smock. He dusted my back. "How's your face?" I asked.

"Your kisses would fix anything."

I percolated inside. I loved this man dearly, with enough lust to kindle a fire.

"My thigh still hurts," he suggested.

I shoved him playfully. "We need cold showers."

"Together?" he asked, hopefully.

I shook my head.

Buzz reached down for his hat and put it on. I picked up the towel and my blunt instrument.

"You've been drinking, Buzz."

He shook his head, perfect denial, but where was the surprise, the shock?

"I haven't had a thing, Carol."

My body throbbed, charged with the kisses, but I was too single-minded for an affair. I lacked any refined skill at duplicity. I also loved Chad and any hint of disloyalty from me would bump his occasional insecurity into permanent paranoia.

"You haven't had a thing this morning," I qualified.

Victor clattered by with his cart. He looked studiously forward.

Buzz lightly held both my hands. "I don't regret our moment," he said softly. "and I'm going to make damn sure you never do either, Carol."

He kissed my forehead.

I grabbed him and hugged him with all my might. "Suzanne saw you drinking the kitchen sherry," I murmured.

His body stiffened in my grasp. "Big Red gave that to me as a Kringle present. He didn't know about me," Buzz said miserably. "He wanted me to try it."

"Buzz, when you kissed me, I tasted alcohol."

He pulled away. His blue eyes looked shattered, like marbles baked in an oven. Shaking his head, he backed into the kitchen.

As jealous as I might be, I wished the heavens would part and a gorgeous damsel in a flaming chariot would swoop down to rescue this shining knight in distress.

CHAPTER FORTY-ONE

When Victor pushed by his empty cart, I called to him.

He jumped. "Ay, chingado," he muttered. "I didn't see nothing."

"It's not that," I said. I waved him into the bakery.

"First Buzz, now me," he teased.

"I thought you didn't see anything."

He smiled sheepishly and then the Tootsie Roll eyes dropped to the towel on my table.

"You're here early," I remarked.

He stared at the towel, his strong face contorting with curiosity. "Is that cabron kid. He's home sick."

"What's the matter with Abundio?"

"Cold, flu, his hair, his freckles, his como se dice." He pointed a stubby finger at the terry cloth. "Wha's that, looks like baby caca?"

"That's some apple that Buzz spit out."

He shrugged as if to say gringos were past figuring.

Fair enough since I couldn't figure myself. Why had I screamed for Buzz to spit out the apple?

"I bet they screw me and don't get nobody to help me," Victor griped. "Do you wanna bet they screw me, Carol?" He thrust out a hand for a wager.

I was distracted by the masticated apple on the towel. Obviously, even as Buzz stuck the apple in his mouth, I'd thought it might be poisoned. Did I believe Buzz had poisoned it, and then enacted an elaborate charade? I shook my head.

"Don't wanna bet, huh? Smart lady. They'll screw me."

Did I think someone had spotted the apple during the brief

interval it'd sat there, had dashed off for some poison and a convenient syringe, and then had rushed back to inject the apple, without being noticed. Ludicrous. I didn't know how I'd persuade Carman to test it. Still I carefully folded up the mess and sat it on the wire rack shelf. After all, Carman had planted the idea that the murderer might try to poison me.

Victor's dark eyes watched as though the world had gone mad and he was helpless in the face of it.

"Victor, you know that honey Fortier received?"

"You mean that honey that made me a prime suspect. Course I don't know nothin' about it." He half turned and looked toward the cart in the hall. He clearly wanted to leave, but, in spite of his rough edges, Victor had been raised as a caballero. He wouldn't turn his back as a lady spoke to him.

"Was it some of yours?"

"Carol, I think it was."

"Why? Didn't it have a red ribbon on it?"

"Yeah, sure." He shrugged. "Anybody could change the ribbon. I seen the jar. Jus' the kind I use."

"Did you tell the cops?"

He gave me an exasperated look, but then forgave my stupidity and added, "When Fortier got that present, Abundio came back and me dijo, 'Sheck it out.' I couldn't believe it."

"Did other people have access to your honey?"

"Oh, sure. It's my usual present. Jar to Suzanne for her birthday. Abundio, of course. We live in the same house. I gave some to Esperanza and Delores. And one jar to the jefe."

"Eldon?"

Victor squirmed.

"Eldon?" I prodded, more gently.

Victor tugged an earlobe and kept his eyes averted. "Well, he hired my whole family," Victor said defensively.

CHAPTER FORTY-TWO

The rain drummed and the interview room steamed. Why did people think rain was cold?

Detective Carman listened carefully to my information. "Yeah," he said, "we could send the apple to Sacramento, but we wouldn't have results from the Department of Justice for two or three weeks. It's pretty much take a number and wait." He smiled. "Are you suggesting we look for oleander, again?"

So he did know that I'd made the anonymous call. He realized his error too late. "How'd you know?" I asked.

"That boss of yours . . . the big, puffy guy?"

"Eldon," I supplied.

"Yes, Eldon mentioned that he'd seen you making a call, acting "shifty." I put two and two together, listened to the voice on the recording, and guessed." He seemed proud of his deductions.

With or without the tox-screen results, the apple episode had made me realize how unlikely it was that someone had doctored the honey in the kitchen. Just as no one had sneaked into the bakery and injected the apple with poison, no one would have popped the top on some honey, fussed with mixing oleander into the resistant goo, and tried to put everything back to normal in a busy, peopled, gossipy kitchen. The jar had been delivered for Fortier with the poison in it. I believed I knew who the murderer was and the motive.

As the rain outside slowed to a trickle, I shared my hypothesis with Detective Carman.

He listened patiently. When I'd finished, he thought about it, nodded sagely, and said, "That sounds possible, but how are we going to prove it?"

The big question for me was did I want to prove it.

CHAPTER FORTY-THREE

I'd never been a fan of big holidays like Thanksgiving and Christmas. I preferred less crowded occasions—the Harvest Moon, the vernal and autumnal equinoxes, and January sixth, the last day of Christmas, the day of the wise men's arrival, the Epiphany.

I sang along with Tom Petty on the way to work. I had the volume loud enough so I couldn't hear myself. By January sixth, Christmas sales ended, frantic lines to exchange gifts melted, and Archibald's removed the delightfully poisonous poinsettias (a four, according to *Deadly Doses*) along the wide, gracious stairs.

From the lot to Archibald's, I sang softly, blotting my voice with the jingling rhythm of my keys. I walked in the middle of the road, away from trees and shrubs. Once inside, I turned on lights everywhere before I changed my clothes. I sucked on my sore lip and poked on my cheek to test its tenderness.

Today I was going to bake sesame brioche. I unlocked the refrigerator. The foil cover on one bucket had been knocked off, probably by a cook shoving it aside to clear room for half-used products. My good mood vanished. I'd complain more vociferously. This was the bakery's shelf and I took pains to keep it neat and uncluttered.

I lifted the bucket. Droplets spattered the dough like dirty rain. I turned back to the Use-First shelf. A covered, but raw piece of meat swam in blood. Surface tension amazingly held the red pool in the shallow plate, but even as I watched, a drop escaped, ran a circuitous route around the bottom, and finally let go. If I even breathed on the plate, I'd cause a spill, but I had to see the exact nature of this idiocy. I considered letting the blood spill through the racks to the floor and then insisting to Eldon that the culprit clean it, but sweetness and light prevailed over my black spirit. I stepped out to the garde manger and nabbed one of their towels. I spread it where my bucket had been and carefully lifted the foil over the meat. Blood sloshed over the edge of the plate.

Under the foil was a heart. A big heart. I jiggled the plate to spill more blood, and then, carefully, drew down the platter.

The door opened, the seals sucking air, and I dropped the plate, spraying my shoes, pants and the floor with red. I bobbled a slippery heart, my hands coated with blood.

CHAPTER FORTY-FOUR

"I see you have a heart," Buzz said.

"Very funny." I picked up the empty plate while hanging on to the slick purplish organ with one hand. A smooth slice had flattened one side. I placed that side down on the plate and sat the raw meat on the shelf. "Blood from that thing dripped on my brioche dough." I wiped my hands on my smock since it was already streaked with red.

"That's the kind of stuff I've had to deal with, with Ray on the lead line."

"What kind of heart is it?"

"Beef. What did you think?"

Buzz absentmindedly poked through containers that had invaded my shelf.

"What's it doing here?"

"We had that movie star last night." Buzz glanced over his shoulder. "Michael Weir? Lucky for us, at least some manager or secretary called ahead and said he wanted heart. For the iron."

"I thought people ate liver for iron." I took the already bloodied towel from my shelf and used it to mop blood from my shoes and the floor.

"That's what Eldon asked the secretary: 'Don't you mean liver?' The guy goes, 'No, Mr. Weir doesn't eat liver. Livers strain toxins and should never be eaten.'" Buzz shrugged and opened a large, green plastic bowl. "This is so goddamn frustrating."

"Whatcha looking for?"

"Chicken stock. For the curry. You can see how Ray puts stuff away, and he doesn't label a friggin' thing." Buzz pulled forward a gallon jar. "Here it is." Buzz walked toward the door, but I stomped out in front of him. I wasn't going to clean any more of the mess. The cooks were responsible and I wanted him to know it. I went to change my smock.

Two minutes later, I bolted from the locker room, buttoning my clean smock, an epiphany shining in my eyes. I hadn't locked the refrigerator because Buzz was there, and I bet he hadn't locked it because he expected me to return for the dough. Someone was waiting for this moment. With the door unlocked and Buzz and me in our niches, anybody could enter the refrigerator. And, someone desperately wanted to because that's where the honey was. I knew it with blinding clarity. If we shoved around the half-used quart of chutney, the wrapped wheel of jarlsberg, the gallon of tomato paste, behind those and the white, five gallon buckets, we'd find a small jar of honey, where Fortier had abandoned it after his escapade with Delores.

A natural place. A place where it would blend with the surroundings. Like the purloined letter, right in front of our eyes.

I entered the kitchen through the swinging door, grabbed my rolling pin, and flew toward Buzz.

He saw the weapon and threw up his arms. "I promise I'll make Ray clean the shelf," he said quickly.

I put a finger to my lips, but he continued nervously. "My thigh still has a bruise on it the size of a baseball, Carol."

"Did you lock the 'frig?" I whispered.

He shook his head and slowly lowered his hands.

"Did you hear someone go in there?"

"I might've, but I just assumed it was you."

I crooked my finger and he followed me, wiping his fingers on a towel. I pulled open the refrigerator door.

"Que chingados estan haciendo ahora?"

"We could ask you the same question," I said.

Victor stood with a great deal of dignity in the center of the cold cell, clutching a cheap Styrofoam ice chest to his stomach. He smiled. "Busted."

"What's in the cooler?" Buzz asked.

Victor sat the white Styrofoam box on the floor and squeaked off the lid. In it, ice cubes surrounded a large, white package.

Hanging his towel on my shelf, Buzz wiggled the package from the container, spilling ice cubes on to the tile. "Beef tender?"

"For Esperanza's farewell," Victor said shyly. "I guess that's going to be sooner than we expected."

"Probably." I didn't have to ask where she was going.

"Have you found the honey?"

"I know where it is."

He nodded fatalistically. "We knew you'd figure it out, Carol."

"Put back the meat," Buzz said evenly.

CHAPTER FORTY-FIVE

Victor left, toting his ice chest. He didn't ask whether we'd tell or not. Either he knew we wouldn't, or he assumed he couldn't do anything about it if we did.

"How did you know Victor would be in here?" Buzz asked.

"I didn't. That's not what I expected at all."

The Use-First shelf was at shoulder height for me. I sat down the rolling pin and shoved aside containers.

"Carol, I told you I'd have Ray clean that."

I squatted and peered up through the wire shelf. I picked up Buzz's towel.

"Today," Buzz added.

"There it is," I said gleefully. "Help me, Buzz."

"Help you what?"

I pushed a five-gallon, white bucket full of dill pickles to the edge of the shelf. "Lift this down to my shelf."

"You want me to put junk on *your* shelf?"

"Come on, Buzz. This is no time to joke around."

He obligingly hoisted down the heavy bucket. "What is it time for, Carol?" I handed him one of Ray's unlabeled, plastic, mystery containers.

I stretched on tip toes and fished, my hand wrapped in white terry. I felt the beveled surface of the small jar. "It's time for this."

The Christmas lick-and-stick tag was still on the red and white ribbon around the jar's neck. To: My honey. From: Your honey. The penmanship was feminine and tentative.

The door sucked open.

"You found it," Victor said. "I knew you would, Carol." His

dark eyes pleaded with us.

I quite seriously considered becoming an accessory to murder. When I looked at Buzz, he was thinking about it, too. I supposed we already were accessories having allowed Victor time to make a phone call, although, I rationalized, at the time I had not yet found the evidence.

I sucked on my lip. "She hit me, Victor."

"I yam very sorry about that, Carol." He looked contrite. "She probably thought she could get that honey, as long as you didn't see it, but she got scared with you coming in here every day."

"You knew all this time?"

"I wondered. Ever since that puto got my honey."

"Why didn't you take the honey just now?"

"Oh, I yam not as clever as you, Carol. I didn't know it was here."

Of course not, I thought, but Esperanza did because she knew exactly the type of thing Fortier would do. "Why did she kill him?"

Victor shrugged. "You can't tell your kids who to like. They jus' hate you. I think Delores loved the puto because he was older and she never had a father. He shoulda been her step-father; instead he gave Esperanza money and said, 'Get an abortion.' Well she did," Victor said. "I'm ashamed I didn't kill him then. After that, he still came around. I couldn't believe it. Finally, I put a knife to his throat and he got the message. When he got with Delores, it felt sick. He used to play with her, take her on the swings and buy her dolls and clothes."

I tightened my grip on the jar and picked up the rolling pin. With Buzz there, it seemed unlikely Victor would lunge for the jar, but I wasn't about to have another fat lip. "Victor, this is a tough decision for me, but Esperanza will need a good lawyer."

"She was the only baby Esperanza had left," Victor said, "and Fortier was going to kill her. Not physically, but in the heart." He clasped the left side of his chest as though it ached.

"I have to call the police, Victor."

He smiled. He knew that I knew he'd called, a secret we could never speak. With his knowledge of safe houses, in ten hours or so, Esperanza would disappear into Mexico.

"Is what you have to do, Carol."

CHAPTER FORTY-SIX

Chad and I sat on the back steps. Lola napped in the crushed Peruvian lilies. I held Chad's hand, but the way one foot jiggled and his eyes darted told me that he needed his nicotine fix and that this wasn't a good time to talk. But it had taken weeks for me to gather the courage, and I felt ready now.

"Chad, what would you think if I decided to make a career change?"

"And become a cop?" His voice was almost surly and he retracted his hand.

"No. I'm a little old for that."

He patted the pocket of his flannel shirt.

"They're on the table," I said.

He ignored this. "Let's see. Not a cop, then a private investigator?"

"Sorta."

"Sorta," he repeated, standing. The yard was too small for pacing. He looked through the sliding glass door to his package of Vantage on the table.

"Remember how I mentioned Rat Dog? She traces down deadbeat dads? Maybe I could do work like that. Not too dangerous."

"The way this case was 'not too dangerous'?"

"Esperanza wouldn't have killed me."

"She killed Fortier."

That was the bottom line. Poisoned him. I remembered that summer afternoon with Patsy and Suzanne. The memory stirred up guilt the way nudging beached seaweed stirred up gnats. Had my glib holding forth trickled back to the kitchen? Both Suzanne and Patsy loved to gab. Had I inadvertently planted the idea for murder in Esperanza's head? The doubt and fear swarmed around me, thick, but amorphous. I couldn't bat away the feelings, but I wasn't ready, yet, to voice them. Clearly, though, I needed some productive way to use the plotting, dark part of my character, so that it didn't spill uncontrollably into harm. As though he sensed my emotional turmoil, Chad took my hand again. "Do you think they'll catch Esperanza?"

I shook my head. "No. But she may never see Delores, or Victor, or Abundio. She's lost the most important thing in her life—her family."

"But she saved her daughter. Her motivation was noble," he said. "Not like greed or revenge." He stood again and stretched. "Speaking of noble, I'm going to see a hypnotist."

Inwardly I applauded, but I didn't say anything on the off chance that he meant to see a hypnotist for a reason other than to stop smoking. He kept stretching elaborately, as though warming up to announce his exploit.

"I would have tried hypnotism before, but I hate the idea of losing control of myself."

"If you pick someone reputable, I don't think you have to worry that he'll make you oink like a pig or anything ridiculous."

"It's not that," Chad said with irritation.

Enough irritation that I almost wanted him to go take a puff. All right, I thought, it wasn't that, so what was it? He didn't want to lose control. Well, that was understandable given what had happened to him when he was little, given what his life had been like when he didn't control it. I took a deep breath. "Sorry," I said. I wished my mother were present to witness the moment. She would have collapsed on top of Lola in the flower bed. Sorry was a rare word in my lexicon.

He smiled grimly.

I could see now that the topic of the conversation hadn't really changed. Indirectly, we'd been discussing control the whole time. In his own way, Chad was apologizing for needing to control me, for not letting me go, not encouraging a career change. Pain had made him protective.

And, for once, with the smoking, I'd backed off, released my control, letting him find a solution. I wondered, sadly, if Buzz would find one.

I clapped. "I'm so glad you're going to try this, Chad!" One hurdle at a time, I figured. I had a lot of practical stuff to sort through before I could make career change.

Chad glanced toward the cigarettes on the table and then sat back on the steps. "So what happened with Suzanne and Eldon?" He switched to this lighter subject to distract himself from the cellophane packet.

"Well," I said with enthusiasm, "Suzanne asked Eldon for days off."

"Days off! Whoa! But from what you've told me, wouldn't he just give them to her."

"Oh, he did."

"So, what's the punch line?"

"Suzanne told him she needed the time because she was uncomfortable when her herpes were flaring up. She figured that would discourage his interest."

We laughed together for the first time in weeks. It felt good.

If you enjoyed *Murder, Honey*, watch for *Deadly Plays,* the next Carol Sabala novel. *Deadly Plays* is currently under representation by Harris Literary Agency, PO Box 6023, San Diego, CA 92166.

CHAPTER 1

Thirty teenagers stared at me. They were neither rude nor terribly interested. Alvina Jameson, the teacher, had efficiently commanded the students into two concentric semi-circles before the stainless steel table. I wanted to shoo them back a full step. I could hear one kid's wheezy breathing.

"I thought she'd be a man," a tall boy in the outer circle whispered.

A tiny girl with long, long hair whipped around. "Geez, Chendo, Mrs. Jameson told us her name was *Carol* Sabala."

In spite of the boy's assumption, society had made inroads into sexism. About one third of the cooking class was male. A few of the students were mildly curious about what I was going to concoct with the oversized bowl, flour, yeast, eggs, almond extract, and sugar. I was a little curious, too. I'd made Danish dough hundreds of times, but never in such a small quantity, and never for an audience. Of course, it didn't matter if the recipe flopped, as I'd lugged in a five-gallon bucket of chilled, already prepared dough for the actual baking.

The group hovered with limited wiggling and jockeying, and my admiration soared for Alvina Jameson, who smiled encouragingly at me from the end of the table. I rolled up the sleeves of my chef's jacket, and pushed up the cuffs of the pink turtleneck under it.

"Well, first you take the flour . . . ."

A couple of students found the statement amusing, which disconcerted me. I had not intended to be funny. "I'm so used to mixing dough to make two or three hundred Danishes, that generally I don't measure anything . . . ."

"See, Mrs. Jameson," the tall boy said, "she's a professional cook and she doesn't measure." The boy had hazel, long-lashed eyes stuck in a remarkably clear brown face.

Mrs. Jameson responded with a patient smile, a soft "Chendo," and a finger to her lips.

The beauty of Chendo's skin made him seem nerdy to me. Apparently stepping on a high school campus made one revert to stereotypes.

I hadn't looked forward to this presentation. My boss Eldon had pressured me to come, saying the demonstration would be good p.r. A reporter from the *Register Pajaronian* was supposed to be here, although no such person was in evidence.

I yammered about "proofing the yeast," and smiled when some kid whispered about the muscles in my forearms, the result of years of spiking volleyballs and of stirring batches of dough for three hundred.

I'd agreed with Eldon, the kitchen manager, to come for two reasons. First, it was useless to fight him on issues involving the image of Archibald's, particularly Archibald's kitchen, where I was a baker, actually *the* baker. Second, he'd hinted that there was a "mystery" for me to solve at the school, a possible poisoning that Alvina Jameson wanted someone unofficial to "look into." I was flattered. I'd gained a reputation, at least among the kitchen staff, because I'd solved a murder case, but that had been over two years ago. I'd toyed with the idea of becoming a private investigator, but my husband Chad had been, and continued to be, dead set against it.

Eldon, my immediate boss, was a dichotomy: a boring, born-bureaucrat who blathered at length, as though he had no insight into his audience, but yet was dead-on at reading people. He certainly knew what buttons to push to get me to comply with his wishes. We had, though, compromised on my dress. I had agreed to wear the top half of our uniform, the white chef's jacket and chef's hat, if I could forego the creepy houndstooth pants for regular jeans.

"I don't think that's the right image," Eldon had insisted. "It doesn't look professional."

"I'll believe I'm a professional," I replied sarcastically, "when I get paid like one."

"That outfit would not accurately represent the way we dress at Archibald's."

"How am I going to check out the poisoning for your 'friend' if I stick out like a maraschino cherry?"

His soft face twisted into a moue of disapproval. "*Mrs.* Jameson is *not* that kind of friend."

As I finished the Danish dough and hefted the bowl to Alvina Jameson, I wondered how she and Eldon knew each other. I rolled the already cooled, manageable dough from the five-gallon bucket. The demonstration was going well. When I lapsed into silences, Alvina breezily filled them. "Look, class, at how she rolls the dough. A light touch."

"Do bakers make good money?" The boy who asked was as tall as Chendo, but filled out and beefy. He wore a red cap twisted backwards.

I felt like telling him that every twist of his cap shaved off I.Q. points, but instead I said, "No. I, fortunately, have a husband who works."

"Do you have any kids?" The girl was the one with the Godiva hair who'd set Chendo straight about my gender. She was so tiny only her chest and smooth, soft face showed above the table.

Alvina Jameson shot the girl a look to say the question was inappropriate, but she simply tipped her head of luxurious brown hair, requesting a response.

"I used to," I said dryly, "until I got this new recipe for pot pies." I'm demented; I enjoyed watching her figure it out. Her dark eyes popped. "I'll demonstrate that recipe next time Mrs. Jameson invites me to speak."

Eldon had supplied me with a generous two-quart container of expensive Danish filling, a mixture of marzipan, cream cheese, sugar, and slivered almonds. I brushed a thin layer onto the rolled dough, and cut the dough into sixty strips.

"Do you always have to wear that dorky hat?" the beefy kid asked.

"Javier!" Mrs. Jameson said sternly.

I thought that was a hell of a question given his backward cap, but I kept my voice neutral. "It's either this dorky hat or a hair net." I was glad that he hadn't seen the pants.

"I'd rather wear a hair net," he pushed.

He wanted more reaction. I ignored him, picked up one of the strips and twisted it like a locker room towel for snapping.

"Wow," Javier said sarcastically.

Mrs. Jameson edged close to his big shoulder. It didn't seem possible that she could intimidate him, but he clearly did *not* like the teacher beside him. He turned from her and wilted.

In about one second, I'd wrapped the dough around my forefinger into a Danish. I picked up another and another, fast as a machine, and I could see the kids were suitably impressed. Chendo offered a genuine, "Wow." Showing off, I made Danishes with my eyes closed and then I shaped a few behind my back.

While my adult colleagues found such displays tiring and obnoxious, the kids liked it, and wanted to know what else I could do. After I'd dolloped each pastry with raspberry filling, the bell rang. I was tired and felt the salty, nervous sweat in my armpits, but I had to admit that I'd had an enjoyable time. Maybe I should become a cooking teacher.